Malachi

Leon Michaels

Book By Leon Michaels

"Action/Adventure"

The Path Home

From The Mists Of Darkness

Task Force Nemesis

Tales From The Bench

The Echelon Factor

Today is Yesterday's Tomorrow

The Path They Have Chosen

"Black Ops Series"

Operation Damocles

Operation Dokkaebi

Operation Yofune-Nushi

Operation Kartikeya

The Black Orchid

Operation Heracles

Operation Pandora

Operation Pegasus

The Twenty-First Special Operations Group:

    Book One: Family

    Book Two: Operators

    Book Three: Survivors

"Science Fiction"

The Morbius Expedition

Random Acts of Science Fiction

A Rigged Deck

Willem

The Reconstruction of Cassiopeia

Malachi

Three Against The Darkness

"The Hanover Series"

The Hanover Throne

The Bellus Project

The Bellus Legacy

The Bellus Myth

The Bellus Solution

The Bellus Prophecy

The Phoenix Project

The Bellus Curse

A Lancer's Tale

A Lancer's Journey

Soraya

The Halfling

The Herculin Factor

The Crane Equation Trilogy

The Crane Equation: The Early Years

The Crane Equation: Rebuilding a Nation

The Crane Legacy

Acknowledgements

As always to my Wife of almost forty-eight years for putting up with my late hours, then dropping a manuscript on her to proofread.

To the United States Marine Corps Public Relations people from whom I stole the cover photo. It did not have any photographer listed and I had to take for granted it was from the USMC/PR people considering its content.

The Discovery

From four hundred meters away, Malachi Thoris felt something was wrong as he rode his mare towards the McAlister place. He stopped and took his monocular from his belt pouch and looked at the front of the farm house. The gate was open, which was rare, and it looked as if the front door was also open.

Because of the picket fence, he could not see in the yard very well, but it seemed there were things lying about in what has always been a neat area. He put the monocular away then pulled the Kreger seven millimeter lever action rifle from his scabbard, checked to make sure it was ready if needed, then gently spurred the mare on towards the farm house.

As he closed upon the fence, he saw clothing and books amongst other things strung out upon the grass between the fence and the house.

"Hello the house!" He yelled twice with no response.

Malachi was only sixteen and he would not lie to say he wasn't scared of the situation he had rode into. He carefully mounted the steps to the front porch with his head swiveling back and forth as he listened for the slightest sound.

He took a deep breath and stepped through the front door. As his eyes adjusted to the darker area, he saw how trashed it was. Malachi only stood for the few seconds it took for his eyes to adjust before he slowly moved into the house, trying not to disturb the mess in the floor.

As he passed each open door, he just looked in to see beds overturned and other things thrown about it as he made his way towards the back door. He paused to look into the kitchen pantry to see it was stripped bare.

When he got to the open back door, he felt sick as he saw the McAlister family hanging from a tree in the back yard. He left the house and went to the tree, stopping about four meters from the tree to look at the family hanging by fencing wire around their necks.

Mister McAlister was the only one with clothes on his body while Misses McAlister, Amity, their eleven year old daughter, and Maxwell, their eight year old son were all nude.

Their hands were tied behind their backs and their ankles tied together. There was blood on the inside of Amity's thighs showing she had been raped and teeth marks on her small, immature breasts that looked to have been deep enough to draw blood. He was glad that Amity's blond hair was covering her face as the looks on the others was horrifying in death.

Malachi turned away from the scene, dropped to the ground and vomited until his stomach was empty. He was shaky as he stood up, then walked around the house without looking back at the bodies to his horse. He took his canteen from the saddle horn, washed his mouth out, then washed his face.

He then took his communicator from his belt pouch, and checked to insure he had a satellite connection and pressed the emergency code into it. Seconds later he had a return.

"This is Emergency Services, what is your emergency?"

"This is Malachi Thoris. I'm at the McAlister farm and they are all dead. The place has been trashed."

"Do not touch anything. Rescue Services are being dispatched along with the Marshalls Service."

Twenty eight minutes later a sub-orbital shuttle landed containing Rescue Services. Malachi told them the bodies were hanging in a tree in the back yard and stayed with his mare as they went around the house. About five minutes later, a high-speed aircar arrived with two Marshalls who he also directed to the rear of the house.

One of the Marshalls returned to take Malachi's statement then released him to return home. When Malachi returned home and told his parents about the McAlister's and how they had died, his father only commented a death by hanging in such a manner had to be a slow death, slow strangulation. Whoever did such a thing was cruel and sick of mind.

The next day, Malachi's father dipped into their meager savings and bought newer rifles and a couple of pistols for protection of their farm and persons.

A week later the Marshalls come to Malachi's family farm to advise them that from all the evidence they could collect and shuttle imprints found out in the pasture, it appeared that Raiders had hit the McAlister farm. If it had been Slavers, they would have taken the young girl and boy with them.

The only puzzling thing from this crime scene was why they had hung the family instead of shooting them as was normal in such cases.

Fleet Marines

Senior Lieutenant Malachi Thoris stood watching members of his Infantry Platoon lay out the bodies of the Raiders who decided to fight rather than surrender while other members of his platoon were strip searching the survivors.

A planetary survey drone had detected this base during a fly-by of the planet and Planetary Survey immediately notified the Fleet. Since the drone used passive sensors, it was estimated the Raiders did not detect the drone as being anymore than space junk moving passed the planet.

Malachi's Second Platoon Para-dropped onto the small village during the night during low altitude fly-over of their Assault Boats while First Platoon went directly for the location of three space craft parked nearby.

The fight on the ground lasted longer than Malachi himself estimated even with the superior weapons, body armor and tactics of the Marines. Each hut, or shelter had to be cleared as these people did not want to surrender. Some did pulled back into the jungle only to pop-up in the rear of the Marines as they moved to the next habitat.

Of the thirty-seven men in Malachi's platoon, there were eleven wounded with only three needing evacuation to their transport for additional treatment. Malachi had two Corpsmen assigned to his platoon and one of those was requiring evacuation. He was also one of the wounded, but his wound was just a deep gouge in his right thigh from a very near miss.

This was Malachi's third assault on Raiders since joining the Fleet Marines after the University. As much as it bothered him to see children amongst the dead as they either fought with their parents or just got caught in the cross fire, he could never get the image of Amity McAlister hanging from a tree limb out of his mind, knowing she had been abused as she had been, and alive when she was placed there to die.

Malachi had seen reports on DNA recovered from both dead and alive Raiders that was cross checked against raped females during raids by them, showing men with wives and children often took part in the rapes of females during those farm raids. He could never understand how those men could do such things when they had families.

An Assault Boat was hovering at a thousand meters above them scanning the surrounding terrain for any Raider that might have decided to fall back into the thick vegetation to avoid being captured or killed. From their last report, they had no humans on their sensor screens.

When the boat landed to evacuate the seriously wounded, it brought a five person team from Fleet Intelligence which would process each individual killed for record, then collect any and all documents found within the village. Malachi knew this could take hours, but such was the life of a Marine. Short hours of extreme violence followed by long hours of stand around and wait.

Once Fleet Intelligence had done their thing and the few prisoners they had taken were loaded into one of the Raider's vessels for transport to the nearest Fleet Base for further processing with a prize crew aboard the vessel, Malachi's Marines moved the bodies of the dead into the heaviest wooden structure, tossed everything burnable on top the bodies they could find around the area, then set it on fire, along with the other structures in the village.

When Malachi judged the fire was as good as it was going to get, he ordered his men off the planet and back to their carrier for hot showers, hot food and rest. Except he would not get any rest until his After Action Report was filed.

The Fleet Cruiser Roberts which Malachi was aboard, followed the captured Raider vessels to the Fleet Replenishment Base on Esperanto, retrieved the prize crew once the transfer of ships and prisoners was made then headed for Tantus, the Marines primary base in the region. Malachi's unit had been replaced on patrol, and it was their time for a bit of shore leave. then back to training and replacements in preparation for the next deployment.

Malachi was sitting in the Enlisted Mess as he rarely ate with the officers. One of the reasons was that his men knew they could talk to him if they had a problem or felt something needed done to improve the unit even though Malachi was considered tough on getting things right. They were three days out of Tantus when he had a visitor to his table he never expected.

He watched Senior Lieutenant Darla Smelter of the ship's Intelligence section enter the Mess Facility, locate him then get herself a cup of hot tea before coming to his table. She sat the cup down opposite him then took the chair facing him. Darla was a Hayutan, maybe one point four meters tall with hair almost black as night framing her diamond shaped face and hazel eyes. Other than briefings, Malachi and Darla had never interacted before, which made him wonder what she was doing there.

"What can I do for you Lieutenant Smelter?" He asked as she was getting seated.

"It's not what you can do for me Lieutenant Thoris, it's what I can do for you. I have a bit of information which I felt you need to know."

"Well then, lay it out for me. I'm all ears."

"Lieutenant Thoris, your name popped up when we ran the DNA on the dead you left behind at the Raider camp. It referenced a Marshalls report on the murders of the McAlister family."

She saw Malachi's grip on his own cup tighten as his facial expression never changed.

"Do tell Lieutenant. How did it tie me with the bodies?"

"From the DNA collected from one of the dead men, it crossed checked to part of the semen left in Amity McAlister. He was one of her rapists."

Malachi took a long drink of his cooling tea before speaking. Smelter could see his hand slightly shaking and as hard as he tried, he could not stop the shaking.

"So, partial justice has been served, but you did not have to advise me of that situation."

"Lieutenant, from what we could gather from the records and DNA, the individual who participated in the rape was between fifteen and eighteen years of age at that time. I understand you were sixteen when you discovered them."

"Lieutenant Smelter, that was over ten years ago. Granted it brought me to the Fleet as I wanted revenge, but revenge is a weak attempt to escape reality. I only hope his death was a slow one."

Smelter took a drink of her tea before responding.

"Now I have a personal question to ask you Lieutenant."

Malachi looked at her wondering what was coming next.

"Well, you might as well ask it Lieutenant Smelter."

She smiled and Malachi seemed to detect a slight twinkle in her eyes.

"Rumor is you never interact with any females when deployed. Why is that?"

"Lieutenant Smelter, if you are asking me if I prefer men, no. Never been with one and never felt the need to try one out for size. I'm just not big on ship board romances."

"Neither am I, but once we hit Tantus we both have a week off to rest and relax. Do you have someone waiting for you there?"

"Lieutenant stop beating around the bush and say what you are thinking."

"I'm thinking that dinner tonight here or in the officer's mess, then maybe, if we can come to an agreement, see how well we match up.   Then maybe if things are right, we can spend the downtime on Tantus together. I may be a bit forward here but this is the Fleet where nothing is guaranteed."

He looked at her for a long time, finding his tea had cooled to the point it lost its flavor.

"Alright Lieutenant dinner in the Officer's Mess. Nineteen hundred hours?"

She stood and picked up her cup as she smiled at Malachi.

"Nineteen hundred it is."

He watched her walk away thinking he may have made a mistake, but then again, it had been a long time since he was with a female, and from the way her uniform fit, she certainly was a female. She was right that in the Fleet nothing was guaranteed except for long tedious hours on watch and maybe a violent death. Maybe it was time for him to make some kind of attachment rather than just accepting what came along. But he never considered she might be more than the time she spoke of.

During dinner they talked about various things, mostly about where they were raised, and such. She did tell him that her roommate was working the mid-watch plus was involved with a weapons officer so they would have her room all to themselves until she had to stand watch in the morning, ship time. This meant they would not have to use a room on the Rec Deck for such things giving them much more privacy.

By twenty-two hundred hours, Malachi was wondering if he had strained himself as she was very active in bed and she sounded as their coupling was very pleasing once they completed the first course in bed. She woke him an hour later for a repeat performance. As they lay snuggled face to face before sleep took them both she told Malachi he was her first for this deployment meaning she had been celibate for nearly six standard months.

Darla arranged for her roommate to be away for the next two evenings which gave her and Malachi the privacy they both preferred. They decided to spend the week together especially after Darla told Malachi that she had no intention of allowing things to advance further than hot, sweaty nights, especially with a Marine who lived out on the edge when dealing with Raiders and Slavers.

A day out of Tantus, Darla arranged for quarters at the Fleet Recreation Site in the Tantus Northern Alps. Their days were spent hiking or skiing in the mountains with their nights exploring each other's bodies.

They parted as friends with no strings at the end of the week with the mutual agreement if and only if they found themselves needing a bit of relaxation, they could contact the other one to see if they were available, but also that if another came along, to enjoy that person.

Malachi returned to find himself moved up to Company Executive Officer, with a whole new set of problems to deal with as new men joined the unit with some of the older troops being promoted and transferred to units needing them.

He threw himself into his new assignment knowing if he did a good job he would eventually be promoted to Captain and get a company of his own.

Italia

Italia was a lush, green planet in the Northwest region of the Federation that had been settled over two hundred standard years before. It's orbit and relationship to its sun gave it an almost yearly planting season making it very profitable in the export of food. It also had a modest mineral content, capable of supporting the planet's industrial complex without having to import many metals for processing.

As cities grew with immigration bringing in people skilled in trades required for industry, the chasm between the politics of the urbanite and the rural population widened. Although the freedom of vote was never denied anyone as per the Principals of Leadership which were enforced by the Federation Parliament, the rural inhabitants were becoming grossly out numbered causing problems within the economic structure of the planet.

This imbalance between the two groups had been seen before within the Federation, by the Principles which had slowly been usurped, even at the Throne whose personage was to insure those Principles were maintained.

Complaints were flowing in that deliveries of food stuffs were not being delivered to the cities in sufficient quantities while the farmers and ranchers were claiming they were barely receiving thirty percent of the value for their labors.

Soon the Throne and Parliament had no choice but to send in the Federation Auditing Service to determine the cause and recommend a solution as even the export of food from the planet nearly ceased, putting other worlds within the region at risk.

With nearly two years under his belt as Company Executive Officer, Malachi's unit deployed to Italia as rumor of revolt came to the ears of the Throne.

It was widely broadcast to the population of Italia that the function of the Marines was to insure that no revolt would take place to remove the elected government of Italia and to insure that the Auditing Service could fulfill their mission. If the Auditing

Service determined that the current government should be removed and new elections take place, then the Marines would insure a peaceful transition within the capital.

Malachi's Company landed and took up positions around the planet's Parliament building without incident, but as the Audit was taking place, snipers began taking shots at them and any personage attempting to enter or leave the facility.

For the Marines, the Rules of Engagement were simple. They could not return fire unless they had a clear, visible target, even if they knew a shot came from a specific window in a building facing them. They essentially became targets in a shooting gallery.

The body armor the Marines wore prevented many of the Marines from needing evacuated due to wounds but it was wearing hard on their nerves. Only the discipline instilled into them prevented them from laying waste to the surrounding building to prevent the sniping. But as one older Marine pointed out, ruins also make for superb sniping positions.

It all came to a head after two months when the Auditing Service announced that the Government of Italia was in violation of the Principles of Leadership and by order of the Federation Parliament would be removed and new elections would be held.

What started as demonstrations in the streets leading to the Capital Building soon turned into open warfare. It would be later discovered that a group of wealthy businessmen had brought in mercenaries to prevent the removal of a government that was making them rich by the day. Their purpose was to train volunteers to become a militia, to prevent the removal of the government.

Malachi and his Company Commander agreed the positions they held were not ideal, but they were functioning according to the plan they had been given. As tensions had intensified, Malachi all but emptied the munitions stores aboard their carrier in case any fighting occurred as it would be almost impossible to get even one of their Armored Assault Boats safety into their positions.

It did not help their situation that the Auditing Team refused to allow the Marines to place spotters on top of the capital building as they claimed it would provoke violence.

Just after midnight, two days after the Auditing Team made their announcement, all electric service to the area surrounding the capital building was cut. The Marines who were operating on a twenty percent alert status, quickly moved to one hundred percent and made ready for what they feared would came to them.

It was estimated that an area approximately six blocks around the capital was in the dark but a mistake was made by the other side in that as dim as the lights from even seven blocks away was, it still silhouetted people moving down the streets, staying close to the darkened buildings. That back lighting made the night vision systems of the Marines even more effective.

The Marines watched the windows of the buildings facing them and caught several glimpses of flashlights being used and curtains being removed from those windows. Still they had to wait for the other side to start the dance.

An individual stood at the edge along the top of one building and fired a rocket propelled grenade at the Marines positions. Two Marines had that individual in their optical sights and when the grenade was fired, they immediately returned fire, knocking that individual back onto the roof. The rocket grenade exploded out in front of a bunker, pelting the Marines inside with rocks and such through the firing slit in the bunkers front. The dance had started.

The people who had been moving along side of the buildings rushed the Marine perimeter only to find themselves facing a volume of fire which mowed them down like a scythe through wheat. As this was happening, fire erupted from windows above them with additional rocket propelled grenades being fired at the Marines. The Marines returned fire in kind, hopefully removing as much of the threat as possible.

Even with the fire power the Marines presented to the fight, they were taking causalities as shrapnel from the grenades were finding flesh. They were being attacked from three locations down the streets leading to the capital building.

They had already planned for this and once the shooting started, eight Marines went to the top of the capital building to observe and report on the activity in the streets, especially those that had not been used to attack the perimeter yet. Four of those Marines were snipers who began to play havoc on those using the windows of buildings to fire from as they had a slight height advantage.

Four hours into the fight, just before daylight, an observer reported a group moving up the street which had not been utilized yet. Malachi smiled as he began to see their plan shape up in his mind. If the Marines had sufficient casualties early enough in the fight, they might move troops from the quiet section to fill in thus weakening that part of the perimeter.

There was no doubt they were taking casualties, but only five needed removal to the Aid Station for further treatment, and one of them was a Corpsman.

Even before the attack erupted from the new direction, two of the snipers began making those people pay for their stupidity. Soon they began receiving fire from windows facing that direction and two rocket propelled grenades were fired at the roof top without success as both hit nearly a floor beneath them. Those firing the grenades did not survive to fire a second one.

Once the fight was joined from the fourth direction, things got intense. An Armored Assault Boat dropped between buildings to fire on the attackers only to be hit with shoulder fired anti-aircraft missiles, knocking the boat down onto the street, killing the boat crew, but also effectively restricting the flow of people down the street.

Mortars were useless in this environment which put the mortar gun crews on the line as Infantry. The Marines Phoenix aircraft was also inhibited from being used as they only had ordinance which would have completely destroyed the buildings around the capital building plus the shock and possible shrapnel could endanger the Marines on the ground. But they did fly overhead, causing the attackers to surrender the roofs.

Malachi was moving to one of the positions to get a better view of the attack when he received shrapnel in his left leg and arm from a grenade. He managed to get to his feet and stumbled the last twenty meters to the position, diving into their position to get out of the line of fire.

Just at daylight, Malachi received the report that the Company Commander was down as he was moving to the fourth avenue of attack. His condition was unknown at this time. The men with Malachi bandaged his wounds as best they could while maintaining a volume of fire to prevent a rush on their position. Ten minutes later Malachi was informed he was in command since the Company Commander was dead, plus the First Sergeant was in the Aid Station with critical wounds.

Malachi sent one single order to all his Marines. Give no quarter. When that order was passed, rifle grenades began entering windows that was suspected of hiding snipers and other people intent to do the Marines harm. That had been prohibited until then.

It was late morning that Malachi noticed the volume of rocket propelled grenades greatly slackening making him think they had expended the majority of that weapon. But with each grenade fired, calls for Corpsmen came from near the grenades impact.

When he dove into the position he was stuck in, only one man was wounded out of the four in it. Now three of those men were wound, but were staying in position, doing the best they could under the circumstances.

Malachi knew if they did not get relief soon, they may not last until dark and some positions were reporting seeing Italia military uniforms mixed in with the militia attacking them. He had talked several times to their carrier command advising them of their situation and asking for any help they could provide.

As painful as his wounds were, Malachi refused pain killers but an IV was strung up for him to replace some of his blood loss. As it neared noon, Malachi had learned he was down two platoon leaders, with one killed and another seriously wounded. Also of the nine Corpsmen they had landed with, three were dead and another one wounded but working in the Aid Station as best he could helping those worse than himself.

He was watching information coming in on his face shield via his AI when he received a radio call he was not expecting.

"Gisborne Two this is Canterbury. Hold what you've got, help is one the way, over."

Malachi asked his AI who Canterbury was and it replied the Canterbury was a battalion level transport/assault carrier belonging to the Free Lancers. Mercenaries who worked along side the Marines to maintain the peace.

"Canterbury, this is Gisborne Two, we are holding by a thread. Over."

"Gisborne Two, all boats away over."

Malachi tried to compute the time for the Lancer Assault Boats to transit to the surface but his mind was too over loaded and tired. He put out an all unit call advising Lancers were coming in and to be sure of their targets before firing up a friendly.

The Lancers came in hot firing upon any group carrying weapons as they landed. It was well known that a large portion of the Lancers were former Marines who now practiced their trade for pay. To them, the Marines trapped around the capital building were their brothers and sisters in dire straits.

The fight would last another two hours before the first Lancer was able to gain the Marine Perimeter. With the Lancers being able to maneuver, they pushed hard against the people between them and the Marines, pushing them into the waiting Marines who found the perfect payback for the hours they had put up with under fire. When the militia began throwing down their weapons, it took every ounce of discipline for the Marines to not finish the fight without prisoners.

When the call came for the Marines to cease fire, Malachi seemed to fold within himself as the stress he was under was finally lifted from his shoulders. He was trying to run the numbers in his head on how many men he had lost but he kept stumbling with the numbers even though he could have called up the basic information via his helmets AI.

Malachi heard an open call for the Marine Commander and one of the Marines he was hunkered down with rose up and indicated where Malachi was located. A minute or so later, Malachi watched a Lancer officer step to the edge of the Marine fighting position. The Lancer touched the side of their helmet causing the face shield to move out of the way.

"Lieutenant Thoris?" They asked.

Malachi looked at the face of a blond female Centaurian with the fur on her face removed to give her a blond halo effect. She moved a thin boom mic to her lips then spoke to her AI.

"Elf, full frequency broadcast please."

Malachi could not hear the AI confirm its instructions. Then the officer spoke again.

"Fleet Cruiser Roberts, Lancer Cruiser Canterbury, stand by. Lieutenant Thoris, I am Captain Emmanuel Braxton, Ninth Lancers. You are hereby relieved along with your troops as I now have command of this situation. Lieutenant, in review of the situation, well done sir, very well done. Your Marines have done you proud."

Braxton straighten up and saluted Malachi who tried to return it in his condition.

"Forgive me Captain if I do not stand, but they nearly killed me today."

Braxton called for one of her medics who immediately checked the bandages already applied then without asking permission, hit Malachi with a pain killer injector which knocked him out within seconds of application.

When Malachi awoke, he was in the Medical Bay of the Roberts with his left side bandaged from his ankle to his neck. He tried to move his head but realized he had a nerve disrupter applied to his neck preventing the nerves within his lower extremities from transmitting the pain from his wounds.

He had no idea what day or time it was as his vision was limited because of the nerve disrupter and bandages. Suddenly his bed began to elevate bringing his head up to where he could gain vision to his surroundings. At the foot of his bed was Darla Smelter operating the bed's controls.

"What's the condition of my company?" He asked as she moved around to his head. Darla leaned over and gave him a short kiss before responding.

"Mal, don't concern yourself with that now. Just get healed up, so maybe we can have another night together."

"Darla don't be beating around the bush. If you want that night together, tell me how bad my company was shot up."

Darla pulled up chair and sat down beside Malachi and took his unbandaged hand.

"Mal, the company suffered. Seventeen dead, thirty-two critical wounded but survived which includes you. Only five escaped being wounded and they were up on the roof. Malachi, you have to remember you were put in a bad position by people who did not understand tactics. Then we, the Fleet had no intelligence warning of those people who attacked your position."

"What of Italia's actual military? Why didn't they step in to help put the revolt down?" Malachi asked of Darla.

"The Lancers asked the same question of the Army's Chief of Staff after they took him into custody as being implicated in the violation of the Principles along with most of the government. He claims he never received orders from the Capital and ordered the Army to stand ready, but to not become involved."

"Bull shit Darla, we killed dozens of his men during that fight, maybe several hundred."

"He claims they deserted and went over to join the revolt. The ones that survived the fight are making the same claim."

Malachi just laid staring out into nothing as he tried to get a handle on what he was being told. Neither spoke for a long time as Darla just held his hand. He finally broke the silence.

"Why are you here Darla?"

"I'm off duty, and I wanted to be with an old friend."

Malachi and Darla had met several times since their week together in the mountains, usually for a night, maybe a weekend if the time presented itself. Neither spoke of lovers they had enjoyed while separated, and both knew all they would ever have was those few hours when together.

Even though they had been on the same ship when Malachi's unit was ordered to Italia, they never had time for one another other than a short kiss in passing and a wish you well greeting.

Before either could carry the conversation any further, one of the ship's doctors entered the cubical where Malachi was resting and ran Darla out. The doctor sat down in the chair Darla had occupied so he could talk with Malachi.

"Alright Doc, give me the bad news that I'm out of the Fleet on pension."

"Far from it Lieutenant, in fact unless you do something really stupid, you will be ready to lead Marines again within a solar year. What little damage you received to your bones was from splinters sticking into them. Otherwise you only received soft tissue damage which was easy to repair. You did lose a lot of blood but your Marines kept you hooked to a replenishment system and that is what really saved your life, otherwise the blood lose would have done you in. I've written those Marines up for a commendation."

"Doc, I'm not going to lay here and tell you it didn't hurt like hell until that Lancer hit me with an injector."

"We took sixteen pieces of shrapnel out of your arm and leg. Your torso side armor protecting your ribs showed seven hits which did not penetrate. Lieutenant, to be honest, you were very lucky."

"What now Doc?"

"We're two days out of Tantus where we will transfer you to the Fleet Hospital there so you can heal up and began therapy once you are ready. I know they will warn you there but do not push your therapy as it will only cause problems in the future."

"I understand Doc. Now what about my men? How are they doing?"

"They are well, moral is high from what I have seen, but three men will either be retired or take lesser assignments based upon the Medical Review Board. And they all have been asking about your condition. Let me leave now so Lieutenant Smelter can come back in to visit with you."

"How did she know I was waking up?"

"Lieutenant, she has been here every day since you came out of surgery, sitting, holding your hand and talking to you about every subject under the twin Suns of Sparus. Take it easy, someone will be in to feed you later."

Malachi had to chuckle about the doctor telling him to take it easy as he was confined to the bed, unable to move.

Darla returned and they talked until a Corpsman brought him soup and politely asked for Darla to leave so he could feed Malachi. She came daily to see him and was present when they took him to the shuttle bay and watched him leave the Roberts to transit down to Tantus.

Reassignment

A month after arriving on Tantus, Malachi began his physical therapy to rebuild the damaged muscle in his arm and leg. Darla came to see him every chance she had just to remind him that he needed to get well. When she told him she was once again shipping out, she locked the door to his single occupant room and gave him an oral reminder of what he was missing while laid up.

Malachi took nothing for granted in the relationship he had with Darla as he moved through his physical therapy and several nurses and one female doctor while Darla was traversing space.

He had been promoted to Captain, but had yet to receive orders when Darla returned and in his physical condition at this stage of his therapy, he was allowed to leave the hospital for another week in the mountains with her. But he was restricted from skiing or other activities which might cause a problem with his recovery.

Darla told him this would be the last time they could meet unless he received orders to the Hanover system as she was being promoted and transferred to Fleet Headquarters on Denoyelles. He saw her off at the end of the week as she lifted to a Fast Destroyer which would take her about half way to Denoyelles, then catch a ride on a transport the rest of the way to Denoyelles. Both admitted an affection towards each other but knew it was only the time they spent together and the enjoyment of the company.

Ten months after he arrived at the Fleet Hospital on Tantus, Malachi was given a clean bill of health notating his recovery was better than first estimated to take. At that point, all he could do was wait for orders.

His orders arrived a week later. He was being transferred to the Fifth Marines on Keres for reassignment. His orders left what assignment open at the discretion of the Commander, Fifth Marines.

Malachi sent Darla a message advising her of his orders, telling her as much fun it was being with her, to find someone with a stable life to settle down with. Her reply was for him to do the same.

It would take Malachi four months and three different ships before he arrived on Keres, the location of the Throne. Malachi found himself assigned as the Assistant Operations Officer of the Fifth Marine Regiment based on the Fleet Base of Destros.

Within a week of his arrival, a Regimental formation was held and Malachi was awarded the Federation Medal of Valor for his stand on Italia. He protested the medal as he stated it was a joint plan, not his own and he just executed it to the best of his abilities once his Company Commander was killed.

But as with all medals awarded, the recipient wore them regardless of their personal concern towards actually earning them. The only positive note as far as Malachi was concerned was that it greatly improved his love life as females from all over the Fleet Base were almost throwing themselves at him during the first year of his assignment. He just took things as they came at him and worked hard at his assignment.

Malachi had been on Keres for over a year when he was sent out to observe joint training between the Second Battalion and the Ninth Lancers based on Keres. He was standing on a ridge overlooking a valley watching the combined forces attacking a strong point when he heard a voice behind him.

"Well you're looking a lot better than the last time I saw you Captain Thoris."

He turned to see a blond, female Centaurian whose facial fur had been removed giving her a halo effect to her face. She was wearing the insignia of a Major on her collars and a smile on her face.

"Excuse me Major, I have the feeling I know you but cannot place from where."

She pulled her glove off her right hand then offered her hand to him.

"I'm Emmanuel Braxton, I relieved you on Italia. Considering how shot up you were, I have no doubt you do not remember me."

He took her hand and felt the strength in it which was not all that unusual for her being a Centaurian.

"Major, may I say it is certainly a pleasure to meet you under these circumstances verses the last ones we met under."

She laughed before responding.

"Captain, I'm the new Operations Officer for the Ninth. Just reported in yesterday, so answer me this. How well do you think the combined exercises are going?"

"Major, considering about seventy percent of the Lancers down there are former Marines, I don't see how it could get any better. Since I am only observing, I'm staying out of the communication loop. This is their show, not mine."

Neither spoke for several minutes as they just watched the troop movements in the valley below. Braxton broke the silence.

"Captain, I have been told that you detest that medal for Italia. Being the officer who relieved you of that debacle, let me tell you that your Marines did one hell of a job holding that position against overwhelming odds. From what I have seen and heard about command and control, even shot up, you did one hell of a job maintaining control of your Marines. Once again, well done Captain."

Malachi turned to look directly at the Major.

"Major, did you come up here to observe the operation or to walk me back into my nightmares?"

She turned to him.

"Malachi Thoris, I came here to invite you to dinner at the Lancer's Officers Mess with the intention of convincing you to give a talk to my staff and Company Commanders concerning how you and Captain Portee set up the defenses of the capital building

27

on Italia. But pay close attention to me here, you are not the first and certainly not the last to find themselves holding the line at the gates of Hell. Not only am I a widow, I watched my husband die holding such a line. This is all I have to say on the subject."

Malachi looked into her dark eyes to see the pain that still resided in them, then turned back to observe the operation that was coming to an end.

"What time do you suggest we meet for dinner?"

"Twenty hundred, unless you have a better idea."

"Twenty hundred it is."

Neither spoke until she left Malachi standing on the ridge alone with his thoughts. When he returned to his office, his boss, a Lieutenant Colonel asked him if Major Braxton had contacted him out in the field. Malachi acknowledged the contact and told him they would meet tonight and discuss the possibility of giving her people a lecture on the defense of the Italia Capital. The Colonel just nodded and Malachi went to his desk to clear as much paperwork as possible for the rest of the day.

Due to the distance from where the Marines were billeted to where the Lancers were located, Malachi checked out a tri-wheeler from the motor pool to use to cover the distance. As he started up the low steps to the Officer's Mess, he found Major Braxton, still in uniform, waiting for him. She offered her hand to him once again.

"Right on time Captain, and I see you arranged transportation."

"Yes Major, the distance is a bit stretched out and I'm not going to hump it unless I have at least a platoon pushing me forward."

Braxton laughed then ushered him into the Mess. They had a table near the back of the Mess reserved for them and the waiter was waiting for them. Malachi told Braxton to order for him since he was not familiar with what the Lancers had available to them.

She ordered Antelope steaks smothered in onions with mushroom sauce, with a spiced baked potato, then Blossomberry wine.

As they sipped on the wine while waiting for their dinner, they were interrupted several times by Lancers recognizing him and two former Marine Officers that Malachi had served with when he was a Sub-Lieutenant. It was finally when their steaks were served that they were able to discuss her idea of having him lecture or brief her officers on Italia.

"Captain Thoris, would it offend you if I just called you Malachi during this meeting?"

"Well Major since you are buying, how about just calling me Mal."

Braxton laughed.

"In that case, please call me Emma, which is what my friends call me instead of Emmanuel all the time."

"Emma, it will be a pleasure. Now, tell me what you are thinking in reference to meeting your officers."

She sat a miniature holograph emitter on the table and activated it. What it displayed was the layout of the capital building to include all of the Marines positions.

"We mapped out your defenses once we took over the mission finding them as close to perfect as possible given the manpower you had available. What will most likely happen is that you will field questions on why you set things up the way you did. Plus other questions such as I have but will wait until the briefing."

"Alright Emma, now tell me when you wish this to happen?"

"In three days, our deployed units will be back on Keres and we have five days before their replacements ship out. I would like to do this sometime within the first three days of their return."

"Fine, tell me when and where, and I'll square it away with my boss."

"Mal, I'll submit a formal request through him, that way we keep everything proper between our units."

"Fair enough. Now where did this tasteful wine come from?"

The evening ended as it began with nothing more than a smile and a handshake between them at their table. Malachi turned back before exiting the building to see Emma talking to another Centaurian Lancer officer. It wasn't that he was considering things going beyond what had happened, it was that it had been a long time since he had been with a Centaurian female, and Emma was certainly attractive.

The briefing took place five days later with Braxton opening the meeting with her analysis of the positions and their construction around the capital building on Italia. From that point, Malachi took over what was basically a question and answer period concerning the choices he and Captain Portee made in setting up their defenses.

"Captain Thoris, it seems that you had more heavy weapons that normally found in a Marine company. How did you arrange that?"

"Simple, I raided the ship board Marines armory since they were not going to deploy with us. If they were to drop later, they would not have to bring those weapons since we already had them on the ground."

"Captain Thoris, looking at your bunkers, why did you place Plastron sheeting out over your gun slits? Didn't that restrict your ability to fire above street level?"

"Yes, it did. Our Rules of Engagement also prevented us from engaging above street level. By putting the louvers out over our gun slits, we also prevented snipers from shooting down into the bunkers through the slits, thus protecting our people from incoming fire. Granted we did eventually take casualties from RPG hits in those areas but I believe all in all, we saved more

Marines by doing so. I have to give credit where credit is due in that our First Sergeant recommended the louvers."

"Captain Thoris, I noticed that your bunkers were not connected by tunnels or trenches. Was that on purpose?"

"Not being connected was due to the Auditing Service restricting what we were able to do. It took three days once on ground and dodging snipers before they even allowed us to set up the bunkers. The only good thing was our body armor prevented any hard casualties and their snipers were not very good at leading targets. We brought in the Plastron Sheeting and set it up so our Marines could dig in behind it without having snipers taking them down before the bunkers were built."

"Captain Thoris, from the reports we have seen, once the fight started, except for the men who went to the roof of the capital building. The only people moving from point to point were Captain Portee, yourself, the First Sergeant. Why is that when you had casualties, the areas not under direct attack were not withdrawn to replace the wounded?"

"You forgot our Corpsmen, but the reason we did not fill in with people from other areas was we decided early on that we could not be certain if and when any area of our perimeter would come under attack. Squad, section and Platoon leaders were given the option to move people within their sector to insure the heavies stayed in the fight. We were just lucky that no position took a hard enough hit to eliminate it and require the movement of people into it to get those weapons back in service. Without a doubt, we were very lucky."

"Captain Thoris, do you attribute a major portion of that luck you mentioned to the manner in which your bunkers were constructed?"

"Most certainly."

The question and answer period lasted for over two hours before Braxton closed it off. Once all of the officers had left the room to return to their duties, Braxton invited Malachi to the

Officers Mess once again for an early dinner. As before the dinner was business like and upon departing he left with a handshake and a thanks for the briefing so her people would have additional information to work with in case they found themselves in a similar situation.

Even thought they would meet for dinner two more times over the next three weeks, nothing advanced between them further than the first meeting. But during this time, Malachi began dating a Senior Lieutenant from Fleet Supply with their second date ending in his bed and almost every date thereafter ending the same.

When they had a four day weekend to spend at the Fleet Recreation site on the large Lake Mikhail, Malachi noticed Emma Braxton there with the same dark furred Centaurian he has seen her talking too the first night they had dinner together. But what he noticed the most was her body in a slim bikini showing that parts of her body was denuded of the fur, especially those areas where the most pleasure could be derived from.

Although she was with another Centaurian and they seemed to be enjoying their time together, he never saw a moment of affection exchanged between them. Other than enjoying the view on Braxton's body, he put her out of his mind and enjoyed the woman he was with.

Deployment

The Second Battalion of the Fifth Marine Regiment was in training preparing to ship out when an aircar crash injured their Operations Officer, placing him in the Fleet hospital. The Battalion Commander for the Second asked that Malachi assume that slot and take over Battalion Operations.

Malachi was not sure he was ready for such a step but it did come with the advancement to Major. He was forthright and honest with the Battalion Commander he was not sure he was good enough for the job but would bust his ass to do the best he could. What Malachi did not know was the Regimental Operations Officer had recommended to the Battalion Commander to request Malachi and that he had faith Malachi would perform above standards.

They had five weeks before lifting from Keres and Malachi threw himself into his assignment. A week into his new assignment, he was at his desk when he heard a knock on his door. Looking up he saw Emma Braxton standing in it.

"What can I do for you Major Braxton?"

"You're a Major now Mal, calling me Emma will not be an insult."

"Well good habits are hard to break. What can I do for you Emma?"

"Have dinner with me tonight."

"I have a ton of work here."

"Mal, if all you do is work, nothing will get done, or at least not done right. Take a break and have dinner with me. I'll even say please."

Mal tossed his stylist onto the desk and leaned back to look at her.

"Alright Emma, when and where?"

"Nineteen hundred, Lancer Officer's Mess."

"I'll be there."

She just nodded then left him to return to his work, only he just sat there for several minutes wondering why she wanted to go to dinner with him. It had been over a month since their last dinner, and that was before he had seen her at the Recreation Center with another man. He finally put that chain of thought out of his head and went back to work dissecting the Battalion's Operations Procedures.

When he arrived at the Officer's Mess, he found Emma standing on the steps as usual except this time she was wearing a dress. A pewter grey dress that hit her about mid-thighs, three-quarter sleeves, and with a modest exposure of her breasts. Neither spoke as he offered her his arm, then entered the mess.

They were sitting at their reserved table waiting for their drinks before Malachi finally spoke to her.

"Emma, you look very nice tonight."

"Thank you, I rarely get a chance to wear something other than my uniform anymore."

Before Malachi could ask why she had worn a dress this evening, their drinks were served and as usual for them, she ordered for both of them. Once the waiter left to fill the order, she broke the silence between them.

"Mal, I'm going to be honest with you about why I'm dressed the way I am. I am hoping you will like what you see well enough to make this evening end other than it has during our other dinners together."

Malachi took a sip of wine before responding.

"And how do you envision this evening ending."

Emma never took her eyes from him as she spoke.

"With my dress crumpled on the floor of my quarters and your uniform on top of it."

"Emma, if I may be so bold, that actually sounds like a very pleasant way to end the evening. But are you sure I will not upset someone else by doing so?"

"What someone else? Mal, I've been celibate since my husband was killed over four years ago."

"Emma, then who is that dark Centaurian I've seen you with several times, the one you were with at the Rec Center?"

Emma lightly laughed before answering.

"Mal, that was Winston, my father's younger brother. I often use him to ward off those trying to get into my bed and he uses me as an attention getter to attract females. And it's worked very nice for him."

Malachi put both elbows on the table and cupped his head in his hands as he just looked at her for a moment before responding.

"And you've waited this long to take another to bed and you've chosen me? May I ask why?"

This time she blushed before answering.

"My husband wasn't a Centaurian, and no, I was not a virgin when we met. I do not adhere to the loss of virginity as part of the mating ritual, but he turned my world upside down. I knew when I saw you sitting on that ammo can in the bunker, bloody bandages holding you together that if we ever met again, if it was possible between us, you would have me. I'm not asking for a commitment, just a pleasant evening between two friends which I think we have become."

"Emma, as attractive and I have to admit desirable that you are, I truly never imagined seeing you laid across a bed with me. But you could have anyone in this facility without pause, male or female, so I must ask again, why me?"

35

She paused long enough that she did not have a chance to respond as they dinner arrived. Malachi could tell she was struggling with the answer, but as much as he suddenly became interested in spending the night with her, he wanted to know why him and not another. She finally responded.

"Mal, you're not a Lancer, so I never have to see you die if we were to deploy as a regiment. I can't go through that again. Don't get me wrong, I like you a lot otherwise we would not be sitting here tonight, and if something happened to you as a Marine, it would not be part of a decision that I made that put you in that position. That's the best answer I can give you."

Malachi knew there was more to it, as he remembered her telling him that she had seen her husband die. He decided not to venture any deeper into her reasons.

"Emma, let's enjoy the dinner before it gets cold, then we'll see where the night takes us."

"Alright. One other thing. It seems everyone knows we Centaurian females will take another female when a man is not available, and I cannot deny I have had that experience before I lost my actual virginity, but after I discovered the pleasure of a man, I have not slept with another female since. And I lost my virginity before starting the university. I'm just telling you this in case you might be thinking a threesome might be nice."

Mal tried to maintain a serious look but felt he was failing to do so.

"Emma, I've actually had a threesome and neither female was a Centaurian, but I must say, that was way more work than I wish to repeat. And since I am not into men, there goes that possibility also."

Emma laughed, then cut into her Bison steak shaking her head at the thought of two men servicing her at the same time. With the verbal foreplay out of the way, the conversation turned to their units and then to what books they might have recently read.

36

As they walked to her quarters, holding hands, Mal could tell she was getting nervous with each step they took. At her door, he took her face in his hands and softly kissed her. He could feel her shaking as they kissed.

"Emma, at any time you tell me to stop, I'll stop and never think an unkind thought. I only want tonight to be pleasant for you."

"Thank you Mal."

In her room, he took a quick look to see what was available, and he stopped her from unfastening her dress. He took her hand and led her to a small settee and just sat down with her beside him. Mal never spoke to her as he gently pulled her close and kissed her. It was several minutes before he noticed her shaking had vanished and that her kisses were becoming more passionate.

Soon she was slowly taking his uniform off and as he slid his hand up the outside of her thigh, under her dress, he noticed she wasn't wearing any panties that he could detect.

"Emma, what are you wearing under your dress?"

She giggled. "Only my fur and flesh. Care to see?"

"I think it is time." He responded.

She stood and unfastened her dress and let it fall from her body. As she did a slow turn to show him her body, it was easy to notice that her fur had been removed in her pubis area and around her nipples.

"It can get uncomfortable to have my fur sticky and matted up, or you getting a mouthful of fur at the wrong time."

Malachi laughed and held out a hand, she took it and he pulled her down to him which she straddled his lap. They stayed like that for a long time as she seemed to have lost all nervousness of what was to happen after the years of being celibate.

They stayed like that until she had enough of basic playfulness and made him stand up as she undressed him. He discovered she was talented away from a bed and made her stop before the night was finished too soon.

On the bed, the serious foreplay became hot and heavy as he was in no hurry to complete the process of making love to her. Unlike other Centaurian females he had been with, Emma was in no hurry, and not as aggressive. But when it became time to couple, she proved to be very physical in the act, and very vocal.

As they lay relaxing with her head on his chest, he felt something wasn't right.

"Emma, are you crying?"

"Yes Mal I am, but before you ask, it's because I had forgotten just how great it feels to be made love too."

Malachi just held her as he slowly dozed off, only to be awakened by her fondling him, encouraging him to once more rise to the occasion. The morning was a repeat of night but with him walking her up until she pulled him on top of her.

Later as they showered with them washing one another, she stopped him from washing her pubic region.

"Mal, as much as I might like you to do that, it's very sore and tender this morning from lack of use. May be in a couple of days."

"Do you want me to kiss it and make it all better?" He jokingly asked her.

"Hell no! That's one of the reasons it's in the condition it is in now. But as I said, give it a couple of days?"

"Emma, are you saying you wish to repeat last night?"

"Mal, I have a lot of time to make up for, and since you will be leaving soon…."

He stopped from saying more by pulling her head to his and kissing her. When he broke the kiss, he commented to her about what she was saying.

"I can't think of a nicer way to spend my off duty hours before we lift. My hours are crazy right now, but if I miss a few hours sleep, it'll be worth it."

"My schedule is open except I have to observe a night fire display tonight. After that I'm all yours." She replied.

The next weeks were long for Mal as he worked hard getting things lined out from his new position as Battalion Operations Officer, coordinating with Logistics to insure their bunkers on their troop carrier were full according to the Battalion Commanders requirements.

Emma spent most of those nights in his quarters waiting for him to come to her and even though for a short time things were hot and passionate, she made sure he rested for the next day. Many nights it was nothing more then being together, the closeness of two people who knew time was short.

Neither spoke words which would lead the other to think what they had was more than the moment before them as the days counted down to his lifting.

As large as they were, Fleet Marine Troop Carriers were designed and built to land and deploy their Marines directly out of a dozen hatches if need be, or they dropped them via Armored Assault Boats from orbit.

The Carrier Fitzsimmons was loaded and ready to go. Mal was one of the very last to load as he spent hours checking to insure they were leaving nothing behind. Emma had taken the day off and spent each hour with him even if she just stood out of the way as he dealt with whatever came across his desk.

At the access gate to the landing pad for the Fitzsimmons, they kissed one last time before he slung his shoulder bag and started the five hundred meter to the ship. His bags were already aboard, waiting for him in his quarters. At the ramp, he turned and waved to Emma. She returned it and just watched him disappear into the massive ship.

"What happens now Em?"

Emma did not have to turn to know her Uncle Winston was standing behind her.

"Live goes on my dear Uncle, life goes on."

"So are you going to be standing here when he returns?"

"Winston, they are scheduled to be gone for a year working along the Western fringe. In case you haven't heard, I have orders, and will leave this place next week. I seriously doubt I shall ever see him again."

"Why is that Em?"

"Because he is too much like Gilbert was. He'll go in Harm's Way even when he does not need to be there because it is in his nature."

"You're in love with him, aren't you?" Winston asked.

Emma turned towards her Uncle, stepped to him, rose up and gave him a kiss on his cheek. She never spoke to him in response as she turned away and walked back to her tri-wheeler to go back to her office and close out her work before she lifted off Keres.

Ramstein

While Malachi was in transit to the Western Fringe of Federation space, Emma Braxton was transiting to Lancer Headquarters on Hanover to teach at the Lancer Officer Academy. She had arranged this prior to taking Malachi to bed the first time, knowing if he turned her down, she would be putting as much distance, space between them as possible.

But she had judged Malachi correctly in that he would take her to bed, but only if she made the move cause he would never take the step. As with her late husband, she had to take the step as he was too much a gentleman, even though he seemed to have plenty of lovers, but from rumor and observation, they chased him, he just never ran very fast.

Malachi had been gone a month before he sent her a message, telling her to leave her shell and explore life with other men. He expressed as best he could how enjoyable their time was together, but as an old friend once told him, nothing in the Fleet was guaranteed, and from observation it held true for the Lancers.

Where a Marines electronic messages might show a ship, base, or planet they were sending from, the Lancers long ago had simplified their system which would never show their actual physical location. So when Malachi received her response, it did not show she was in transit at that time.

Emma told Malachi that he had set a high standard for a lover in her mind but she would keep the option open to enjoy another if the situation presented itself. And he was to put a smile on some lonely female if one crossed his path.

They would correspond about once a month as his tour took him from one planet to another, resupplying Marine Detachments on some planets, and surveying others for possible bases in later years. He never told her of an Altairian Med-Tech he had been keeping a smile on her face after they came together four months into the cruise.

41

Sevens months into his deployment, Malachi and the Second Battalion found themselves transiting at high speed towards a newly opened world due to an upheaval in the political scene on the planet.

Ramstein sat almost on the furthest edge of the Western Rim of the Federation, having been opened to settlement less than two years previous. The planet was rich of soil for farming and had a healthy supply of metals and minerals according to the original survey.

According to the Federation Settler's Authority Rules and Procedures, off world industrial complexes could not enter a new world and claim vast sections of land to exploit them for off world gain. Ever partial had to first be claimed by private individuals, operated for a minimum of five years at a profit to the claimant, before any consideration of selling it to another, and even then, the land must be privately held for ten years from date of first claim before it could be sold to an off world investor.

Any claim that could not support the owner, could be surrendered back to the Settler's Authority for one half of the original claim fees. Annual audits of each claim was made to insure the claim was viable to the land owner.

The trouble came from land owners who wanted to sell out to off world investors at a profit. Ramstein did not have a Federation Embassy at that time, so there were no Lancers or Marines to provide protection to the Settler's Authority's offices and personal.

Of the two Federation Marshall's assigned to Ramstein, one had been killed by an unknown shooter, and the other was jumped by several men in the dark and badly beaten.

The Second Battalion was the nearest Federation asset to the planet and was order there at best speed to take control of the situation. To calm things down as gently as possible.

The Fitzsimmons was four days out of Ramstein when they received the word that despite the best efforts of the fledging government, the Settler's Authority offices were burned down during a riot. It was commented in the report that the individuals who rioted against the Authority, seemed to be a larger crowd than possible considering the immigration flow onto the planet.

Malachi was sitting in the Fitzsimmons' conference room along with the Command staff of the Second Battalion and the Command staff of the Fitzsimmons considering their options upon arriving in orbit around Ramstein.

He had hard copies of intelligence reports laid out in front of him plus his pad showing the lay-out of the Ramstein Space Port. Malachi had tuned out most of the conversation around the table as he studied the reports. His thoughts were interrupted by his Battalion Commander.

"Malachi, you're about to chew through that stylist, what's on your mind?"

"Colonel Morgan, I know I'm not an Intelligence officer, but none of this makes sense to me from a tactical standpoint."

"Explain yourself."

"Here they are on the fringe of known space, with Raiders operating all through the quadrant, yet they act as if they are throwing away any measure of protection by their actions. By being an Independent world, they would not have any measure of Fleet protection unless a ship happens to be within a parsec of the world."

"Yes Major, we can agree on that. Go on."

"Based upon this incomplete report of the riot where the Settler's Authority building was burnt down, the group involved seemed to materialize out of no where and was mostly well fit men involved. Take into the estimate of the size of the crowd versus immigration reports from the past six months, I would be willing to believe most if not all of those men did not pass through immigration."

"Major, that is something we are looking into at this time." Commented Lieutenant Commander Whitfield, the ship's Senior Intelligence Officer.

Malachi just nodded as he continued to look at the papers in front of him.

"Malachi, why do I think there is something you have not said yet?" Colonel Morgan queried.

"Commander Whitfield, do you have access to the Survey satellites still in orbit over Ramstein?" Malachi asked.

"Certainly. What are you thinking?" Whitfield responded.

"Everything we have here, visual wise is almost two months old, I don't like the idea of dropping in blind."

Whitfield went to work on his pad to establish a link between the Fitzsimmons and the satellites. It was only a couple of minutes before he advised Malachi of the satellite situation.

"Major Thoris, there are eight satellites over Ramstein in Geo-synchronist orbits, but only three will respond." Whitfield reported.

"Please display all." Malachi instructed.

A holograph appeared over the table with the active satellites in green and the dead ones in red. It quickly became obvious that someone had blacked out the satellites covering nearly two-thirds of the planet with the satellites covering the space port and regions around it still operational.

"Commander Whitfield, how much definition can we get with the satellites in reference to ground targets?" Malachi asked.

"We can read the nametags on a uniform with them." Was the reply.

"Let's see the space port, to let's say about a half kilometer outside the fence."

A few seconds later the view changed giving the room a view of the space port and the vessels on the ground. Malachi studied the image for a minute before addressing the ship's Captain.

"Captain Brockton, if we were to set the Fitzsimmons down on the port, where would you place it?"

"About as close to center as possible. Federation Space Port Regulations require that area be free of vessels and reserved for Fleet vessels." Brockton answered.

"What are you thinking Malachi?" Colonel Morgan spoke up.

"In checking Port Regulations, Captain Brockton can order the port vacated giving the Fitzsimmons unlimited berthing. Would anyone like to bet the moment he makes the call, we find out that at least two of those ships are disabled and incapable of shifting their locations until repairs can be made."

Brockton worked on his pad for a moment then transferred the information he had worked up onto the holograph. He sequenced it for several seconds, then as the Fitzsimmons settled into the center of space port within the simulation, first one then another of the grounded vessels exploded.

"Malachi, was this what has you worried?" Brockton asked.

"Yeah Captain, and I can see it happening even if we do a combat drop to secure those ships. Colonel Morgan, I cannot in good conscious plan an operation to secure the space port. I see too many unknowns in this operation."

Morgan shifted in his chair giving him a direct line of sight to Malachi.

"Alright Major Thoris, you have followed form, now unplug the Book of Regulations out of your ass and let's get this show on the road. We have been ordered to the surface and unless we can prove otherwise, we have to make the drop. But no one said we had to drop on the space port. Let me hear your thinking Malachi."

Malachi wiped the holograph then reloaded the view of the high plateau fifty kilometers to the West of the space port, putting it between that location and the capital.

"This plateau is more than large enough to establish a base for the entire battalion plus support, but we need to get there and offload the ship as quickly as possible, then get the Fitzsimmons back into orbit."

A plan was devised where instead of dropping the Battalion in relays via their Assault Boats, the boats were going to be max loaded with supplies. Each boat would take a position on the plateau which allow the boat to provide covering fires if needed plus support with rations and ordinance for that part of the perimeter.

All surface vehicles would be preloaded to include the Engineer equipment with additional material to establish a base of operations. The trick would be to get the holds emptied as quickly as possible without exhausting the Marines and Fleet Engineers at the same time.

Then once the holds were empty, the Fitzsimmons could lift back to orbit while the stacks of materials and supplies could then be dispersed and bunkers constructed to protect them. Also the Assault Boats needed to be dug in leaving their top turrets exposed to provide fire support to the trench line still needing to be dug between troop bunkers.

As complicated as it sounded to an outsider, the Marines knew what had to happen in what sequence to make everything work out as quickly as possible and without excess labor. Both the Battalion's Engineers and the Fleet Engineers had the heavy equipment to handle the earth moving in short order.

A day out of Ramstein, the Fitzsimmons sent the order for the space port to be vacated, cleared of all vessels. As suspected, the three vessels on the pads were reported to be under repair, incapable of lifting.

Just over a half day ahead of the Fitzsimmons were two of its high speed shuttles running under cloaks transporting Malachi and two sections of Marines prepared to para-drop between the space port and the capital. They were going to drop in and collect any individuals leaving the space port.

The drop went as planned with the satellites under the control of the Fitzsimmons thus denying anyone on the planet from observing the para-drop.

Soon afterwards, a dozen Marine Assault boats overflew Humphries, the capital of Ramstein then as they aproached the space port, they began to dump chaff in case there was an attempt to shoot one or more of the boats down. The road to Humphries suddenly filled with vehicles and men on foot leaving the space port expecting the Assault Boats to circle back and land on the space port.

Except the boats flew on for fifty kilometers and set their Marines down on a plateau, dominating this portion of the planet. Upon landing they formed the basis for their base on this world instead of utilizing the space port.

Five kilometers from the space port, the civilians fleeing the location ran into the road block which Malachi had set up. With Malachi was a Fleet Intelligence Officer who took the DNA of each individual and compared it against outstanding warrants and such to determine who was who in this rebellion.

One group of men tried to run, then turned to fight, pulling hidden weapons from their clothing. The fight only lasted seconds considering they were fighting against hardened Marines, not militia.

Interrogation of the survivors of that fight confirmed what Malachi had feared. The port was rigged to blow, to destroy their primary transport or even the Assault Boats if that was all that landed. Marine Engineers landed at Malachi's position and

47

walked to the space port with one of the rebels who said he could show them how the charges were placed to blow the sitting space vessels.

Malachi was sitting in the back of an Assault Boat reading the reports from the Engineers who had disarmed and dismantled the explosive devices aboard two of the three ships sitting on the space port pads. The math showed that even if the bunkers on the Fitzsimmons did not blow, the shock wave from the two small craft would reach Humphries, causing massive damage to at least half of the city facing the space port.

Just as he was about to sign off on the report then order the road block cleared and for his Marines to join up with the Battalion, Senior Lieutenant Farwell, the Fleet Intelligence officer entered the boat to talk with him.

"Major Thoris I have something that might interest you."

Malachi looked up from his small work desk.

"What have you got Lieutenant Farwell?"

"One of the people who we identified as having warrants against them also has a connection to you Sir."

"How so Lieutenant?"

"The McAlister family from your home world. His DNA was found in the young members of the family and on the mother. Also his DNA was found on another family murdered on Birmingham. He was tried in a Birmingham court via his DNA and found guilty of rape and murder, and there is a standing order for his execution."

With Raiders moving from planet to planet, the court systems had developed a manner of trying a Raider's DNA, thus placing warrants and even execution orders against the Raiders.

Malachi just sat and thought for a long moment with Farwell breaking the silence.

"Major, we double checked the individuals DNA twice to ensure no mistakes and it is confirmed. The Saint's has placed this individual into your hands since you are the senior Fleet officer present."

"Are there any others?"

"Yes Sir, but none are tied to you Sir."

"Lieutenant Pennbrook!" Malachi called out.

A Marine Lieutenant stepped into the boat.

"Yes Sir."

"Lieutenant Farwell has identified individuals which have execution warrants against them for actions against Federation citizens. Form a firing squad and finalize the orders of the courts. Lieutenant Farwell, I'll deal with the one you mentioned personally."

"Yes Sir." Both officer's acknowledged their orders.

Lieutenant Farwell followed form in reading the warrants against the men as they stood in front of the Marines formed for the firing squad. He turned the detail over to Pennbrook and seconds later three men met their fates with Marine bullets in their hearts with the fourth man watching the events.

Malachi walked up to the man.

"I'm Malachi Thoris from Henderson. I found the McAlister family after you left them hanging in a tree with wire around their necks to slowly strangle them after raping the youngsters. You have a warrant against you allowing me to execute you but unlike your comrades, you'll not die from a bullet."

He turned away to a Marine Sergeant.

"Sergeant, grab three men and being this bastard along."

As then men followed Malachi towards the tree line, they noticed he was carrying a length of coiled wire and a vibra-saw.

When the Raider noticed what he was carrying he struggled against his captures.

At the edge of the tree line, Malachi picked a sturdy tree then went to another and cut it down, then sectioned off a piece about a half meter tall and about fifty centimeters across. He had the Marines tie the man's ankles together and as he fashioned the wire into a noose, the man began to protest.

Malachi spoke to him as he set the noose around the man's neck.

"The old Earth Bible speaks of an eye for an eye. Amity McAlister was barely eleven when you raped her then hung her with wire like this instead of giving her a quick death. You hung her younger brother after he had been anally raped along with the parents in the same manner, each suffering as it took them a long time to die. No you son of a bitch, you'll not die quickly as you do not deserve it."

Malachi tossed the wire over a sturdy limb then set the piece of wood up on end. He told the Marines to stand the man on top of the wood, stretched the wire as they held him in place, then anchored the wire.

With his hands secured behind his back and ankles tied together, the man was tiddering on the top of the wood, trying to maintain his balance. Malachi placed a medical sensor on the man's chest which was used to monitor injured patients as others were being treated. It would register the man's heart beat then send a warning if the heart stopped beating.

Malachi sent the detail back to the road block and told them to get ready to lift as he stood looking at the man struggling to stay on the block.

"You picked this life and now you shall reap what you have planted in unfertile soil. The warrant of execution against you will soon be accomplished and in that time, I hope that you suffer as those you murdered in this manner suffered."

Malachi walked away as the man screamed at him to shoot him and not let him die this way. Malachi just ignored his pleas as he walked back to the road block. No one spoke to Malachi about what he was doing as Lieutenant Farwell had briefed the Marine Sergeants concerning the events Malachi discovered in his youth.

It was almost twenty minutes later that the sensor alerted that the subject was under duress which Malachi figured he had finally fell off the block of wood. It was almost fifteen minutes later that the sensor reported end of life. Malachi waited for nearly an hour before he sent the Sergeant and a detail back to the subject to retrieve the body and have it buried in an unmarked grave with the others.

As Malachi watched dirt being shoveled onto the grave, he finally determined that he had came to grips with that part of his past and looked towards a brighter future without those memories haunting him. He never thought to ask why they had hung the McAlister's, but it no longer mattered. Almost as soon as the last shovel of dirt was thrown on the graves, the Marines lifted to rejoin the Battalion in their positions on the plateau.

Marines accepted firing squads as a fact of life and duty especially on developing planets as long as proper legal form was followed, and the judgement had been judged as fair. They never commented on Malachi's version of justice as they were shown photos of the McAlister Crime scene by Lieutenant Farwell.

Lieutenant Farwell signed off on the notice of execution forms only stating that one was hung by the neck until dead.

Unpredictable Events

All communications off Ramstein had been blocked and a Scout Boat which had been attached to the Fitzsimmons send an uncoded noticed that the space port had been destroyed along with the Fitzsimmons as it was landing.

Long before they had made planet fall, plans were made for just this situation and as predicted, the Fleet ordered all ships within the region to converge on Ramstein. But what was unknown was that Scout Boats were scattered all over the sector, waiting and watching for Raiders to cross into Federation Space.

Less than a fourth of the sectors Fleet converged on Ramstein as the rest took up positions to move on any Raiders entering to take advantage of the absence of Fleet protection.

Four days after the fake orders to converge on Ramstein were issued, the first Raiders moved into Federation space towards the planet of Memphis and the gold and silver mines located on the planet.

Ten Raider vessels and nearly five hundred Raiders hit the ground to find themselves trapped as Scout Boats and Viper fighters ate into the Raider's vessels until the Frigates they were supporting arrived and finished the job.

The Raiders on the ground found they were trapped with Marines landing, forcing the Raiders into the mines as a manner of protection except the miners themselves fought back with what they had including laser drills and explosives. The Raiders soon discovered they could not withstand the punishment they were enduring knowing their only manner of escape was now nothing more than debris in orbit around the planet.

Another smaller raid was stopped that hit the planet of Peru for the cattle being raised there. The survivors told during interrogation that they were to return with at least four bulls and as many cows as possible so they could raise their own beef to support their operations.

It would take over a year before all of the intelligence on the raids and Ramstein came together. In the meantime, Malachi and the Battalion were running anti-terrorism operations on Ramstein since it was reported by the captured Raiders during the space port operation that there were still Raiders on the planet.

Here was were the Psych Docs had their work cut out for them as they learned that different groups of Raiders had joined together and those they captured were from one group but were not aware who the others were in case of capture. Some of the Raiders were operating in plain sight of the Marines but unless they committed some action against them or the civilians where they could be identified, the Marines were chasing ghosts.

The Fleet had restricted activity at the Space Port to incoming and outgoing cargo in order to maintain the economy as best they could. No new settlers were allowed until the problems could be rectified and no one was allowed to leave the planet just in case those individuals were part of the problem yet still undetected.

Marines were operating off their base on the plateau, patrolling, often raiding once they had viable intelligence of a Raider cell working in an area. They were disrupting activities which if the remaining Raiders had just stopped and thought about it, the Marines would leave allowing them also to leave and return to their bases.

There was a road from Humphries to the plateau. Malachi's Operations Bunker was on the reverse slope of the gentle ridge along the plateau, away from the road entrance to the base. A half kilometer from the Marines perimeter was a check point to prevent any vehicles to just roll up to the perimeter which was a rarity given that the Marines did not welcome visitors.

Contact between the Marines and the Ramstein government had been via video links or specific personnel flying into Humphries for a meeting. Fresh food such as vegetables and some meats were purchased from an open market with the selection of said items taken at random and tested for poisons.

Malachi was working on a plan to raid a settlement far to the north when he heard the call from the checkpoint that a ground vehicle was approaching. It had been weeks since a vehicle had attempted to approach the base and Malachi was interested whom it might be. He left the bunker, and walked to the top of the slight rise and looked towards the checkpoint.

He was watching the vehicle approach the removable barrier blocking the road when suddenly the Marine who was standing at the edge of the barrier was shot by gunfire from the vehicle, then a rocket propelled grenade was fired at the guards bunker. The vehicle sped up and torn through the barrier, heading towards the perimeter.

There were Assault Boats dug in on both sides of the road at the perimeter and they had long since established the routine of traversing with top gun turrets towards the road block when a vehicle approached.

The vehicle had barely cleared the barrier when both boats opened fire on the vehicle. Seconds later it exploded, but this was not a chemical explosion as if it was loaded with normal explosives, this explosion came from a nuclear device which was armed and one of the personnel within the vehicle holding onto a dead man's switch. The man was killed, releasing the detonator and detonating the nuclear device.

Malachi had his face shield down watching under magnification when the device detonated. His face shield blanked out to prevent his eyes from being damaged from the flash of the device but the expanding shock wave of the device picked him up and blew him back and over the top of his own bunker. He felt his body impact the ground, bounce, then hit the top on an Assault Boat that was dug in on that part of the perimeter. The turret of the Assault Boat stopped any further travel of his body, but he was unconscious before he impacted the turret.

Even as the debris was starting to fall from the explosion, the nearest Corpsman to Malachi responded to the call from the Assault Boat he was on and pulled him into the boat then laid out the single Med Bed, placed him on it, then told the pilot to lift him to the Fitzsimmons immediately. The Corpsman grabbed the med packs from the boat and left it as the ramp was coming up as the pilot began to power up for the lift.

Because of the Corpsman's instructions, Malachi would be the first of over a hundred men to be lifted to the Fitzsimmons for treatment with dozens more being treated in the Battalion Aid Station which was also on the same side of the ridge as Malachi's Operations bunker.

The Fitzsimmons had a dozen Repair Tanks also often called Lazarus Tanks and because of Malachi's rank and injuries, he was placed in one soon after arrival in the Fitzsimmons Medical Bay.

Soon the Fitzsimmons tanks were full and others were transported to other Fleet vessels orbiting Ramstein with four Marines put in stasis until another ship could arrive to tank them.

The Battalion's casualty count was fifty-three killed with one hundred and nineteen injured requiring medical treatment from minor, walking wounded injuries to those requiring the tanks.

It was estimated that the yield of the device was just over a .5 kiloton device but the terrain played in it's favor as the shock wave swept up the hill, crushing the bunkers which the Marines were hunkered down in. Except for Malachi and six others caught out in the open, the majority of the injuries came from the collapse of the bunkers. The nature of the device reduced the risk of radiation poisoning.

The top of the Command Bunker which was on the device side of the ridge was blown off with only minor injuries to the Battalion Commander and his staff in the bunker at the time.

Two companies of Marines were dropped from the Frigates in orbit to fill in for those evacuated due to injuries. Charlie Company Commander was elevated to Operations Officer to replace Malachi.

A month after the nuclear event, a Fleet Hospital ship took orbit and all individuals needing further care or in tanks were transferred to it for transport to the Fleet and Marine base on Tantus.

On Tantus, Malachi just floated in a silver sea of nanites as they repaired his broken body while Psych Doc's entered his subconscious mind to insure he could return to duty without trauma.

It was estimate that it would take two years to return his body to it's last physical form. During that time he was given information and at a point his subconscious mind began interacting in sims based upon technology discovered by the Federation's Marshalls decades earlier.

A year into his treatment, Malachi began to attend simulated Senior Command Courses in preparation for his advancement once he returned to duty.

When word reached Hanover of the nuclear attack on the Marines along with a casualty list, a candle was lit for Malachi for his safe return to life as he was once known to the individual who lit the candle.

Learning Curves

With the advancement of the Lazarus Tank technology, no longer was a subject just fed information, they actually attended classes as if they were not in the tank. This was through simulations which gave them contact to both real people or simulated people introduced into the programs.

The connection to the computers while inside the tanks was via nanites which connected themselves to the cerebral cortex of the subjects. The nanites had no control over the subjects as they acted as the link between the subject and the massive computers running the simulations.

In this, the subjects mind was awake and responded to all stimulation during the programs. They could feel what their simulated body felt, hear and see everything as if they were in a real life situation. If they stubbed their toe in the simulation, their actual body felt it.

Based upon the results of Malachi's scores within the simulated Command Course, which had been proven over the decades to be as accurate as if a person was being tested in a real classroom environment, Headquarters, Fleet Marines, requested he be held in the tank an additional six months beyond his release date for further training.

Malachi was in fact a test subject for a training program to better prepare him for future assignments. In the outside world, a day was just that, a day, but within the tanks simulated worlds, a day outside could be a month or more for the subject.

Within the program, Malachi was assigned as the Battalion Executive Officer of an existing Marine unit. In the program, he was released from medical treatment, the tank, given thirty days leave to readjust to being back in the real word, then reported to duty.

By using an existing Marine unit, it was estimated the subject would not realize he was in a simulation and act accordingly. During the time Malachi would be in the simulation, he would be exposed to everything that a Battalion Executive Officer might face to see how he reacted to those matters and the decisions he made. He would also be interacting with people, again, some real, some simulated.

At one point, Malachi took command of a split Battalion as the Battalion Commander had the other half during a deployment to put down a rebellion on a newly settled world. Another time, Malachi had to take command of the Battalion when the Commander was wounded during another deployment.

It was during one deployment that the Battalion was linked to and reinforced by a Battalion of Lancer, mercenaries, on another world being contested by anarchists. The Lancers had attached a Liaison Officer to the Battalion in the form of a female Centaurian Captain.

Malachi quickly took notice of this officer in that she was what Centaurians called a cinnamon, except her shade of red was light, similar to what was once called a Strawberry Blond on Terra. Her facial fur had been removed leaving her a sort of halo around her face. Her exposed neck was clear of the fur as were her arms. Malachi had learned from experience, many Centaurian females had their fur removed from their face, neck, and the front of their bodies so they could also enjoy the fur of a Centaurian male when making love, plus they found they also enjoyed the heat and feel of a normal human during the act.

Three months into the operation, the Captain caught Malachi in the officers showers as he was finishing up the day. It was common practice for males and females to share such facilities and no one gave it much thought. Malachi had his back to the entrance, scrubbing the grim from the day off and never saw her enter.

Her name was Simone Cortez, and she smiled to herself as she disrobed to also clean the day from her body. Instead of turning on a shower head for herself, she went to Malachi, and gently touched his shoulder. He turned to see her standing before him.

"Can I do something for you Captain Cortez?" He asked thinking her already knew the answer.

"Certainly Major. You can call me Simone and then let me wash your hard to reach places then you can wash mine."

The grin on her face spoke volumes where her hard to reach places were located.

"Not going to happen Captain."

"Why not? You don't like what you see?"

"Captain Cortez, or whatever your name is, as realistic as all this seems, none of it is real."

She reached up and pulled his face to hers and kissed him, then stepped back from him."

"That wasn't real? This body isn't real?"

Malachi took a moment to rinse the last of the soap from his body then stepped away from the shower to the bench where his towel was lying. He began to dry off as he looked at her, still standing under the water.

"Captain Cortez, Simone, I am very much aware this is a training simulation and that maybe you are a real person introduced to it, but no further contact between us is desired."

Simone stepped from under the shower towards him but stopped just outside of arms reach.

"Major Thoris, this is interesting. First of all my name is actually Simone Cortez, I was a Lancer Captain before I contracted Paulsen's Syndrome and was placed in a tank. I'm a Doctor, a Medical Doctor or I once was and now I have training and experience as a Psychotherapist. How do you know this is a simulation?"

"Doctor Cortez, I've seen more action in the past year than I saw prior to getting injured and place in a tank. Then there are things that just doesn't ring true, but to be honest, I'd have trouble describing them to you. So let me ask you this, what were your intentions when you entered the showers?"

"I think I made my intentions quite obvious. I wanted you to take me to your bed and relax for a time."

"Now that's interesting. Can a person have such interaction with another, either real or simulated and feel the pleasure of said action. I certainly felt that kiss."

"Yes Major, even as you float within the tank, your mind and body would feel, enjoy the interaction of making love."

"Interesting. Now is this part of my rehabilitation?"

"Yes it is. And to complete the explanation, I would feel every bit of such an exchange as I would if I was in your bed, away from the tanks."

Malachi stood looking at her thinking about cause and effects of such an exchange with her.

"Simone, I know of Paulsen's Syndrome and I'm really sorry that you have that disease. I suspect this is the only interaction you can have with others because of the nature of the disease. But as attractive as you are, no, not today or tomorrow."

"Again, I'll ask why not?"

"Because being a simulation, others are watching, taking notes and I'll not be someone's entertainment through a small window."

Simone walked back to her things, picked up her towel and dried off as Malachi finished his drying then getting dressed. She put her robe back on then moved back to him.

"Malachi, part of my purpose in this is to observe and determine your mental state. Yes, sexual interaction between us would tell me much about your mental state, but it is not necessary at this point. A few years ago, before I became ill, a good friend of mine, another Centaurian told me if I ever crossed your path to make sure that I stopped and enjoyed that time with you."

"Emma Braxton?"

"Yes, Emma."

Malachi finished dressing then stepped to Simone, pulled her to him and kissed her, this time making in a long, hot kiss before stepping away from her.

"Another time, another place having you laid out on my bed would have been nice. I'm sorry Simone."

"So am I Malachi. Even in my current condition, it would have been nice."

Malachi left her standing in the shower room and exited into darkness as the simulation came to an end.

He awoke to a white ceiling and sitting upright in a hospital bed. It took him a minute before his eyes finally focused and looked around his environment.

Sitting a couple of meters from the foot of his bed were three people. One was a Fleet Marine General, another was wearing a white lab coat telling Malachi he was probably a doctor, then the last man was dressed in a business suit.

Malachi tossed the cover off his body to find he was nude, then tested his ability to move as he swung his legs off the side of the bed. The floor was cold to his feet as he carefully stood up. Once up he stretched before taking a step towards the room's window. His legs were shaking in holding him up but three steps later he was at the window, moving the blinds out of the way and looking out at the world beyond the glass.

He turned to the gentlemen sitting in the room.

"Alright gentlemen, since I am not in a sim, I must be out of the tank. Who's first?"

"Major Thoris, how do you know you are not in a sim?" Spoke the man in the suit.

"Excuse me sir, your name?"

"Conrad Harrington, I'm chief programming engineer for the Lazarus Tanks."

"Well Mister Harrington, before I got blown half-way across Ramstein, I knew I was soon due for an optical adjustment as my eyesight was changing. But within the sims, I could see better, and farther than I knew normal eyesight should allow, plus I could read fine print that even when my eyes were considered perfect, I could not read without a magnifying glass. Your computers were compensating and adjusting my eyesight for whatever I was looking at. Just now looking out the window, there was a limit to what I could see. That was just one item that led me to believe I was in a sim."

"Major Thoris, I'm Commander John Marcum, Chief Psychologist for the Rehabilitation Programs. Even knowing that you were in a sim and knowing you could interact with the opposite sex, why didn't you take Captain Cortez when she offered herself to you."

"I thought I explained that to her, wasn't you people watching?"

As Commander Marcum was responding, Malachi carefully moved back to the bed, moved onto it and covered himself back up.

"No Major, anytime one of our patients engages with either a real person within a sim or just a fabricated person, we shut down all visual and audio contact to the sim and only observe the medical readings in case we have to terminate the exchange due to the patients condition in the tank. Yes, we did know what she was attempting to do, but killed all those feeds as she entered the shower facility."

"Does she know you do that?"

"Yes, she does."

"Then Doctor Marcum, why didn't she advise me of that?"

"Major, that is a question we have no answer too."

"Interesting. So what happens now?"

"Major, we'd like to ask you a few questions before the next step is taken with you. For your information, you are the first subject to take part in the last sequence of the simulations where you were in the position of a Battalion Executive Officer."

"Ask away."

For over an hour, Malachi responded to questions from Harrington and Marcum noticing the Marine General just sat quietly listening to the exchanges. Harrington focused on the simulations, especially what Malachi detected that gave him reasons to suspect he was actually in them. Marcum asked a pointed question of why he continued to interact in the sims once he realized he was in them.

"Doctor, it's simple. I figured it was just part of the Command Course training. Every day within the sims, I learned something. I had no idea how long I had before being removed from the tank, and it gets very boring in there."

Malachi looked over at the General who had not spoken a word the entire time that Malachi had been awake. The General's nametag on his uniform said he was Briggs. Malachi had a faint memory of hearing about a Colonel Briggs but not a General Briggs, then he figured he had been out for a long time.

"General Briggs, you've sat there patiently during all of this without saying a word. Not to be rude Sir, but what is your purpose in all of this?"

Briggs looked at the others and spoke to them.

"Commander Marcum, Mister Harrington, after listening to Major Thoris' responses, I think we can safely say the only thing wrong with him at this point is that he needs something to do besides sat around a hospital. Do you gentlemen agree?"

Both men agreed with the General who then turned to Malachi.

"Major Thoris, once the good doctor gets you processed out of here, you will report to the Twelfth Marines and assume command of the Battalion."

"Sir, I've never heard of the Twelfth."

"That's because until you take command, they do not exist except on paper on my desk back on Hanover. With the expansion of the Federation's universe, there is a need for more Marines as there is also an expansion in the Fleet. The simulation you were in gave you time and training as a Battalion Exec, and you proved to be an excellent administrator in that capacity. You have proven time and time again to be a solid tactical and strategic thinker and officer. The time in simulation has been accredited as time served in the Exec's position, so we, the Fleet Marines, are promoting you to Lieutenant Colonel as of today, then you will have transit time to Keres where the Battalion will be formed."

"Manpower Sir?"

"We are stripping the other Battalions of officers and senior non-commissioned officers to form the nucleus for the Twelfth, while the training Battalions are pushing troops through as fast as they can without neglecting training. Some of your Sergeants and junior officers will be freshly minted at the rank you receive them."

"How much time do I have to get them ready Sir?"

"Hopefully you can have them ready to deploy in eighteen months or less."

"General, I'll make you no promises considering where I am currently sitting without seeing the people themselves, but you can trust that I will do everything I can to have them ready and able to fight when the time comes."

The General stood, walked over to Malachi's bed and offered his hand.

"You'll have your orders in hand by the end of the day Colonel Thoris, and good luck."

The General left followed by the other two men. Malachi lay in bed thinking he had best get his legs under him, so he got back off the bed and wandered about the room, looking in every drawer and closet, finding clothing fitted to him and his uniforms ready to go except without any rank on them.

Two hours later, his orders were delivered by a Marine Captain along with rank insignia plus tabs showing the Twelfth Marines. He squared away his uniforms and waited. It wasn't long before a Medical Corpsman entered his room and advised him he probably needed to eat and escorted him to the Mess Facilities. Malachi could only smile to himself that even though he was in fact hungry, as he often did when deeply in thought, he ignored his stomach as he worked on a problem. Only this time, the problem was whether or not he could fulfill the hopes of the General and the Fleet.

First Formation

Malachi was not alone when he boarded the Fleet Marine Assault Carrier Beauregard for the transit to Keres. He had thirty-seven seasoned Marine Officers, Sergeants, and enlisted men joining him for the trip. Men who would become part of the Twelfth Marines. Also on board were forty fresh out of Recruit Training Marines heading for the Twelfth and their first assignment upon completing their basic training.

Before the Beauregard left orbit, Malachi gathered all personnel in the hanger bay to speak to them.

"Marines, I am Lieutenant Colonel Malachi Thoris, the Battalion Commander for the Twelfth Marines. Before any of you start asking me about assignments with the Twelfth, forget about it. I have no idea what Marine Headquarters has on their mind about assignments and our Adjutant is already on Keres awaiting our arrival. Until then I'm the only person who knows what their job will be and that's as good as I have been informed."

He paused to let that sink in before continuing.

"I see a First Sergeant in the ranks so here it is. We have almost six weeks transit time. First Sergeant, I place all enlisted men under your command and control during this transit. They will conduct physical training and weapons training. Check with the experienced men for specialties such as mortars as an example, and cross train every man, including our Officers in them."

He paused again.

"I've already checked with the ship's armory and they have weapons to train with from our sidearms to the crew served weapons found in a Battalion. First Sergeant, training starts at zero seven hundred tomorrow, ship's time. Officers on me, First Sergeant attend to the rest. You're dismissed."

As the First Sergeant was bellowing, ordering the men to the far end of the hanger bay, the officers gathered on Malachi.

"Gentlemen, again, I have no idea your future assignments with the Twelfth but pay close attention to what I told the First Sergeant. I want you gentlemen to be present at every training session and if you are not aware how to deal with a specific weapon, then get your hands dirty and learn it. I'm giving you a six week jump on the officers we'll marry up with on Keres. Take advantage of it. If one of you have advanced schooling in a weapons system, notify the First Sergeant and assist if necessary. Any questions?"

A Captain wearing the nametag Pettigrew spoke up.

"Colonel, my orders are to be your S-4 Sir, your logistics officer."

"Well that takes care of one slot then doesn't it Captain. Now besides PT and weapons training, you will pull a copy of the Twelfths Table of Organization and Equipment (TO&E) from the computers and take a hard look at it comparing it to our manning roster. Make sure some pencil neck at Fleet Headquarters has not shorted us in equipment."

"Frack, I should have kept my mouth shut." Pettigrew announced which drew laughter from the rest of the officers.

"Gentlemen, you can ease up on the laughter as all of you will assist Captain Pettigrew in his assignment. This will help you familiarize yourselves with what the Battalion has available to it. But do not worry as I will also be involved in PT and be looking at our TO&E. Before we get to Keres, we'll all sit down and compare notes. Any further comments or questions?"

He gave them a few moments before dismissing them. Looking across the hanger bay it appeared that the First Sergeant was breaking the troops down into groups. You didn't make First Sergeant in the Fleet Marines without being able to think on your feet.

Malachi decided to go to the Officer's Lounge to grab a cup of hot tea and maybe a pastry if available and just relax until possible need. In the lounge there were swing out computers on all the arm chairs which could be used to read books from the computer storage banks, watch a movie video, or even do your work or monitor your work from the lounge. He pulled up the TO&E for the Twelfth and was going over it when he was joined in the chair next to his. It was the Beauregard's Executive Officer who was female and moderately attractive.

"Colonel Thoris, I'm Kendra Griffin, the Exec here on the Beauregard. I was busy in Engineering when you arrived. Welcome aboard."

Malachi took her offered hand and felt the firmness in the flesh of her hand. This told him she was not afraid of getting dirty even if he did not feel any callouses.

"Thanks Commander. It appears the ship yard did a fine job rebuilding the ship."

"Yes they did. We were down almost two years being refitted. We took one hell of a beating just off the Pacifica Sector. We were a year in space dock before we were able to take her down to the ship yards themselves. They did a great job putting us back together."

"So Commander, is this business or just conversation?"

"I was wondering if you would dine with me tonight in the Officer's Mess, say nineteen hundred?"

"I'll be there just for you."

She laughed as she stood, then walked over and filled a mug with tea and left without looking at him as she passed. He just watched her walk by then turned back to the computer and picked up where he was before she spoke to him.

Dinner was pleasant with talk about each other's childhood and places they had been while in service. From her questions, it appeared she knew much about his past, especially Ramstein even though she never brought up that action. He walked her to her quarters and said good night without touching each other.

Two nights later they were repeating the previous dinner when she finally spoke her mind.

"Malachi, I follow an old rule to never sleep with one of the crew I'm assigned too. I also never sleep with any members of the Marines we carried into battle. But this is a shake down run and you are just cargo if you do not mind me using that term. I do not sleep with women and it has been nearly a year since I felt a man next to me on the sheets. I was wondering if you would like to share a shower with me."

Malachi cut off a piece of the fish he was eating then dipped it into the tarter sauce before forking it into his mouth. He never took his eyes off her as he chewed then swallowed the bite. Before he answered he took a sip of the white wine they were allowed with dinner.

"Your quarters or mine?"

"Mine as it is closer to my post if Battle Stations are called."

"Then once I finish with this meal because the sauce is delicious, I think we need to insure no spot is left unwashed, don't you?"

She just smiled as she took another bite of her salad.

The rest of the transit time was often spent in her bed, even if he just stopped by during the day for an hour when she was pulling a night shift. Malachi learned he was not the only member of the Twelfth enjoying company as it seemed the ship's crew was engaging with the Marines, including those fresh from Basic, including the female Marines.

As Kendra explained to him during the fourth week of the transit, they were not hauling the Marines into battle and everyone was relaxed since they were well into Federation Space and not moving along the Rim where Raider's might pop up at any given moment.

A week out of Keres, the Beauregard slowed down enough to dispatch a shuttle and allow it to catch up as they retrieved the Twelfth's Battalion Sergeant Major that was posted on Wingate with a Depot Security Detachment as their First Sergeant. Malachi quickly learned Sergeant Major Beckett had been with him on Ramstein with Bravo Company as their Gunny.

"Colonel Thoris, it's good to see you Sir. I would have sworn when they pried you off that Assault Boat you were a goner."

"Sergeant Major, I understand if they had waited until the boat that lifted me up to the Fitzsimmons had waited for other injured Marines, I would have been gone. Those minutes saved my life. Now, it seems you have made out fairly well since I remember you being a Gunny."

"Yes, Sir, no rest for the wicked Colonel. Now, what have you got on your mind about this new command?"

"Sergeant Major, you and I are going to lay back and observe then once it all comes together, we give a gentle nudge where needed, or apply a heavy boot where needed. Just hold back until I tell you too, or in case you find a situation that gives you no room to maneuver to keep someone from getting hurt. Got it?"

"Got it Colonel."

Malachi just stayed back and observed as he made mental notes of the training being conducted in the hanger bay. He had passed the word to the Sergeant's that they were not to interrupt training if he came to listen in since this was more important than stopping the classes and acknowledging his presences.

They landed on Keres at midday with Malachi and Kendra having a final night together. Malachi and his Marines exited the Beauregard from the port side, Cargo Bay Three access ramp with Malachi, Captain Pettigrew, and Sergeant Major Beckett leading the men off the ship. Off to the side of the ramp were a group of Marine officers waiting for their Battalion Commander.

At the bottom of the ramp a Major separated from the group, saluted Malachi then offered his hand.

"Colonel, I'm Walter Prescott, I'm your Exec, Sir. May I introduce you to the rest of your staff."

Prescott introduced a female, Captain Alicia Wolenski, who was the Battalion Adjutant. Malachi looked at the Captain thinking there was something familiar about her. Next was Major Thomas Dunlap, the Battalion's Operations Officer. Then Senior Lieutenant Michele Laca, his Communications Officer. Prescott advised Malachi that his Battalion Intelligence Officer had yet to arrive as the transport he was on along with nearly one hundred Marines was diverted to assist a disabled freighter and they were a day out from Keres.

Malachi introduced Captain Pettigrew the Logistics Officer then Sergeant Major Beckett. He told the group he'd sit down with them one on one once he got settled in and learn more about them, but for now they needed to get to their new quarters and get to work.

As everyone moved towards their ground transports, Captain Wolenski asked for a moment of Malachi's time.

"Colonel, my Admin Chief and three clerks has your office set up for you and are awaiting your arrival. If you would allow me Sir, I would like to board the Beauregard and make contact with my sister Sir, just to say hello as we may not have time before they lift in seven days. Sir I have a tri-wheeler for my personal transportation."

"Certainly Captain, take an hour as things won't get crazy until tomorrow anyway. What does your sister do aboard the Beauregard?"

"Sir, she's the Exec. Lieutenant Commander Griffin."

Malachi then knew why she looked familiar even if there were many differences between the sisters in appearance. Wolenski caught the look on Malachi's face of discovery.

"Sir, the name difference is because she enlisted under our father's name while I took mother's maiden name."

"Well that is not uncommon. I was wondering why you looked familiar as I have dined with Commander Griffin on several occasions during transit."

Wolenski gave him a knowing smile, saluted, then headed up the ramp. Malachi watched her walking up the ramp for a moment, smiled to himself thinking if she was like her sister, then put the thought out of his mind as he was not going to sleep with a member of his Battalion. Especially with a female whom he would be working so closely with.

Once Malachi ensured his bags were in his new living quarters, he went to his new office to find it had three stacks of folders on it for his review and or signature. Lying in the middle of the desk was an open folder containing his Assumption of Command document which he signed, then set aside as he got comfortable in his chair and took a folder off the nearest stack.

Most of what he was seeing was housekeeping documents for his attention to keep him appraised of what had been happening as he transited to Keres. He read each page to ensure he was aware of what was or had been happening and initialed off unless it required his signature.

Malachi was reading a file when a Marine rapped on his doorframe. He told the Marine to enter and finished the paragraph he was reading before looking up at the Marine centered on his desk. The Marine wore the rank of Lance Corporal and was neatly turned out.

"Can I help you Marine?" Malachi asked.

"Not really Colonel, I'm your driver, Sir. Your ground vehicle is outside, all maintenance is current on it and ready when you are Sir."

The man's nametag said he was Phillips.

"Well Lance Corporal Phillips, what is your given name?"

"Kenneth or Ken Sir."

"Why don't you grab a cup of coffee, find yourself a place out of the way in the outer office and make yourself comfortable until I feel the need to go someplace."

"Yes Sir. Colonel I am given to believe you will also have a runner and a communicator assigned once the full Battalion is on the ground. Shall I fix up a place for us to loiter while waiting for you to find something for us to do Sir?"

"Lance Corporal that sounds like a superb idea. Also make yourself known to the Sergeant Major so he does not try to insert a boot into your back side for just sitting around. But a suggestion, find a manual on a subject you feel you are weak on and study it while waiting."

"Colonel, I shall do that Sir. By your leave Sir."

"Dismissed Marine."

Malachi smiled as the Marine left his office thinking the young man had no idea what his assignment would entail. But once his runner and commo was assigned, some of the weight of his duties would fade away.

A few minutes later, Captain Wolenski entered his office to deposit another folder and collect the ones he had already gone through especially his Assumption of Command document. He quickly noticed one thing about her that was not present when they first met and that was the fragrance of lilacs. He decided to short stop any idea of interacting beyond duty, especially since he figured her sister had told of their time together.

"Captain Wolenski, a moment of your time please."

"Yes Sir?"

"I hope the meeting with your sister went well, but just in case she spoke of me in terms other than just having dinner together, I do not and will not interact with a member of my command in such a way. The possibility of conflict of interest can always raise it's ugly head even if the relationship is kept professional during duty hours."

"Colonel, for your information, I did ask Kendra about the two of you and she only smiled a knowing smile. I also know she is very selective of her lovers and I will not lie and say that finding ourselves in that situation would not be undesirable, but since you have made your position clear on the subject, do not worry Sir, Keres is a target rich environment for a single female."

"I'm going to take privilege here, Alicia, if I was so inclined, I would consider exploring such a relationship with you, but only if we were of equal rank, and I was not your Commander. One of the reasons is some may think I am using command privilege to entice you onto my bed, which would not look favorable for either of us."

"I understand Colonel. Anything else Sir?"

"No Captain, carry on."

He watched her leave the office thinking another time or place, but she'd have no trouble finding a playmate to spend her off duty hours with. He went back to reading the files.

Later Warrant Officer Lambert, the Admin Chief enters, removes the finished files and leaves without speaking. Malachi smiled that Wolenski had turned that task over to her Chief since his own position on interaction was made clear.

Lance Corporal Phillips rapped on his door again and reminded Malachi it was time for the mid-day meal and that the mess hall would be closing within a half hour. Malachi told Phillips to go to chow then followed him out the door. He found that Headquarters Company Mess Hall was divided into two sections, one for enlisted men, the other for Officers.

Malachi looked at the layout of the enlisted tables then those of the officers and found minor differences, mostly in the condiments and sauces. He located the Mess Officer, a young female Sub-Lieutenant named Torres and asked why the differences. She stated their rations did not provide enough to place on all the tables, so she put them on the officers.

"Lieutenant Torres I can appreciate the problem but let's do this. If there are not enough to go on each table, than either hold them back until a new supply is issued so you can cover all the tables, or place them at the end of the chow line to be used by any that wish them. Do not separate and give the officers anything the enlisted personnel will not receive. Our positions and rank places responsibilities on us that the enlisted do not have along with the additional pay for such duties, but it does not make us any better than they are since they carry the greater share of the physical burden in accomplishing our mission. Do we have an understanding Lieutenant?"

"Yes Sir, a very clear understanding Colonel. Thank you for your guidance Sir."

"Lieutenant, I see no problem in what you were doing as I've seen it all through my career. But this is how I wish things to be and now that you have an understanding, may I say the food smells delicious and I had best feed myself so I can get back to my duties. Carry on Lieutenant."

That afternoon he called a meeting of all of his officers and senior Sergeants along with those of Headquarters Company and laid out a few things he wanted done. He also mentioned the items in the mess hall which he had discussed with Lieutenant Torres which seemed to take a bit of pressure off her from officers wondering why things had changed.

He called for a Battalion formation that evening so he could introduce himself and advise the Battalion of certain things he expected from them. One was physical training starting at zero five fifteen in the morning to include all personnel not on duty, which also meant the off duty kitchen personnel.

Malachi told the Marines the first thing they had to do was ensure the Battalion was physical ready since so many of them had spent weeks and even months in transit to Keres. He called the Company Commanders forward and reminded them to push the physical training according to the weakest individual and build from there. The next morning, he was in front of the Battalion Staff personnel to lead them in the run and other aspects of getting them ready.

The first month was utilized in bringing everyone up to speed physical wise with Malachi often showing up at one of the Company's morning formations and exercising with them. While he was doing that, Sergeant Major Beckett was attending physical training with another company and exchanging information later, usually over breakfast.

It would take seven weeks of evaluating the officers and men before Malachi had a good feel for the status of his Battalion and what needed to be done to fix what needed fixing and only reinforce the rest to keep everyone current and ready to fight.

Into the Field

Four months into his command, Malachi held an Officer's Call for all officers and First Sergeants. He was planning to move to the field to continue training and he intended that everyone got the same word at the same time.

The only personnel that would be left behind were those that the Battalion Surgeon determined were unfit due to injury and not yet ready to return to full duty. Arrangements would be made with the Fifth Marines on Keres to feed and for them to utilize their medical facilities. Those personnel left behind would be the caretakers of the Battalion's area and he would post their responsibilities before the Battalion left for the field.

The Beauregard back swung through on its patrol and laid over on Keres for three days for replenishment. Malachi spent two nights with Kendra on the Beauregard, passing Michele Wolenski exiting the ship as he was going up the ramp to see Kendra. She just smiled at Malachi knowing how he would spend his night.

The Battalion formed by Company with the Infantry in order behind Malachi and his command group. The Weapons Company came next then Headquarters Company. Behind them came the trucks carrying those things the men and women could not carry with them.

Each individual including Malachi was carrying what was called a Field Transport Pack. It was set up for drops in excess of ninety-six hours, and it was the largest pack the Marines would carry.

It was zero five thirty when Malachi turned his back to the Battalion and set off with his radio operator, runner and clerk stepped off in the lead with the Battalion moving behind him in column.

Five kilometers later Malachi turned off the main route to the proposed training grounds. He was taking them cross country which would shorten the trip even as it made the path harder since it was broken ground, untraveled in such a manner.

The vehicles turned with them, slowly following the troops as they moved across the countryside. When they came to terrain which gave the vehicles difficulty, everyone pitched in to insure the vehicles could transverse the ground or creeks. The Battalion's Engineers stayed busy building crossings with the help of the Infantry.

Malachi stopped in time for the field kitchens to set up and ensure the Marines had a hot meal before bedding down for the night. The kitchens were set up in the open without tentage with night watches posted.

They spent two nights bivouacking in column formation before they finally arrived at the site Malachi intended for their base camp for training. He allowed them to settle in for the night in column then the next morning they picked up and moved into a defensive perimeter and began digging it.

The location was next to a forest which covered over a thousand square kilometers of forest which Malachi designated as the central point from which an aggressor would attack from.

Lieutenant Commander Henry Longbaugh, the Battalion Surgeon, who had also marched the distance with his medical staff who were not required to drive the vehicles containing their hospital and equipment or the six field ambulances belonging to the Battalion, reported they only lost one man to the march who had stepped into a hole and twisted his ankle. Longbaugh reported that man should be back to full duty within a week.

As the Battalion was digging in, removing trees near the perimeter, pushing the forest back as they used the timber to build their bunkers and gun positions, patrols were set out as part of training.

Malachi had overflown this area in an aircar and knew it was allocated to the training of Marines and Lancers by Lord Mikhail, Protector of Keres soon after the Fleet Base at Destros was established. Within the forest were cleared areas where obsolete vehicles of various types and sizes were set for targets for mortars and other weapons of those training in the area.

The mortars were still digging in when the first call for fire was sent to them as the first patrol found a target as per their mission orders. Using seeker heads on the mortar rounds with the patrol lasing the target, the first round impacted as designed then the patrol pulled back and returned to the perimeter.

Once the guns were fully dug in and a survey party confirmed their locations, standard mortar rounds would be used instead of the seeker heads due to the cost of those heads. This would require detailed navigation by any patrol utilizing map and compass plus confirming the location via GPS satellites overhead. Malachi did not want his people solely depending on either the seeker heads or satellites since the supply of seeker heads would be limited and satellites had been known to fall from the sky.

Facing away from the forest, the Marine Engineers build a track on which a target vehicle could be pulled by another on a long cable so the crew served heavy weapons could fire upon it day or night. The towing vehicle had a flashing red light on it so a gunner could see it through his sights and know that vehicle was not the target. The target did have a bright light which strobed as if it was firing upon the perimeter.

Once the perimeter was complete to Malachi's specifications, training was nearly around the clock with physical training still a part of the daily business of training. Malachi could be found in any position during the day or night either observing training or often taking part in it, especially the live fire exercises.

A rifle and pistol range was established and platoons were cycled through it daily to stay proficient in their weapons.

Every thirty days, the Company's would pick up and rotate putting a different Company facing the forest even if the Company's opposite the forest were running patrols in it. No one was exempt from the training as even the Medical Staff was required to spend time on the ranges and even did recovery patrols to return simulated wounded or dead Marines back to the perimeter when their units were not able to deal with the problem.

Malachi pushed the Battalion hard for nine months but not as hard as he pushed himself getting them ready. He had been in command for just over thirteen months and felt the Battalion would be ready to deploy before the eighteen month allotted time he had been given.

Sergeant Major Beckett reported that morale was high within the Battalion and if they weren't ready now, they soon would be. Malachi looked at the Sergeant Major and told him they'd soon find out.

Three days later a Lancer Assault Boat landed inside the perimeter, discharging a team of Sergeants whose mission was to insure all live ammunition except for mortar ammunition was retrieved and securely locked up, then blank ammunition passed out to the Marines of all ranks. This was because the Lancers were dropping a full platoon deep into the forest to play war games against the Twelfth.

Malachi kept looking at the Lancer First Sergeant thinking he had seen him somewhere before but could not place him. It finally got the best of him and he approached the First Sergeant who happened to be a Centaurian.

"Excuse me First Sergeant, I have this odd feeling we've met but I cannot place where."

"Colonel Thoris, in case you missed it, my name is Winston Nottingham, I'm Emma Braxton's uncle."

"I thought you were an officer?"

"I was until there became a need for a First Sergeant and I took the job. Besides, it's a lot more fun being a First Sergeant than a Major."

Malachi stood watching the distribution of the blank ammunition for a minute before speaking again.

"First Sergeant, how is Emma doing?"

"Colonel, she is well. She is up for promotion to Lieutenant Colonel and is on Hanover teaching at the Lancer Academy. She lifted a week after you did and from what I have been hearing, she'll stay on Hanover for a while longer."

"If you speak to her, let her know I wish her well."

"Colonel, we communicate about monthly and I will certainly let her know you send her good wishes."

Malachi turned to Winston and offered his hand.

"Thank you First Sergeant, now I'd best get back to work."

"May the Saints protect you Colonel."

Malachi just nodded and walked away not seeing the smile Winston had on his face knowing what Emma would be asking him once she found out they had met. He went back observing his people at work then three hours later lifted to get out of the way before the war games began.

Late that evening, the Lancer platoon that were to be an opposing force dropped into the forest with the Marines going on full alert for two hours then on a fifty percent watch from then on.

The blank firing adapters for all of the weapons were attached in place of silencers and they had an internal microswitch which activated a small pulse laser when the gas pressure of a fired blank pressed against it. This included all weapons from the pistols to the Heavy Two CM guns. Everyone, Marines and Lancers, wore sensors to detect being hit with a laser shot and sent that information to a controller computer for later accounting. It also told the wearers AI if they had been wounded or killed in action.

Malachi pulled a fast one on his own Battalion by having the links to the satellites and drones blocked preventing Battalion Operations from being able to see if anyone was approaching. His reasoning was they depended too much on electronic measures and what would happen if those measures failed.

Then he did the one thing no one could have predicted, he boarded an aircar and left the area placing the Battalion Exec, Major Prescott in command for the duration of the war games. Before he left his comments to his staff was plain and simple.

"People, we have been training day and night for over a year. But here is something we have not done and that was to train to fight without me. Remember I'm just a Marine, another in a long line, and this is your final examine to see if I have properly trained you to fill my boots in case a bullet finds me. I learned on Italia when I lost my Company Commander that I wasn't really ready to take command, but I muddled through it because we had kept close communications between us."

He paused for a moment.

"There is no pass, fail in this final examine, only results telling all of us what needs to be worked harder on in the future. I have faith in each of you to do a good job."

"Colonel, what are you going to do Sir?" Major Dunlap, the Operations Officer asked.

"Major, I'm going to Lake Pilar and do some fishing. Unless the Headquarters observers shuts the games down before schedule, I'll be back in two weeks. As the old saying goes, the ball is in your court, play it."

With that he left the Command Bunker for Lake Pilar. Lake Pilar was a man made lake utilizing the concrete debris when the alien city of Destros was razed by filling in the Southern end of a valley and allowing rain water to fill it. The lake was named after Lord Mikhail's first wife from the Keres' city of Sunow and as it filled, fish from Lake Mikhail was taken to it to stock it for future generations.

Some thought what he was doing was insane but he had made his pitch to Marine Headquarters and they understood his concerns. Malachi had complete faith in his staff, but this was their chance to shine. If he had done his job properly, they would indeed shine.

Privately Malachi believed he had pushed his luck as far as any human could push it and was uncertain if he would live to retire. But the Marines was all he had in his life even with the comfort he found from time to time with the women he had met in his life, they were never there long enough for him to discover if there might be something beyond the nights on satin sheets.

There was a Fleet Recreation Resort on Lake Pilar like the one on Lake Mikhail but for the two weeks he was at the resort, he managed to avoid several entanglements with females both military and civilians who came looking for a good time or a husband, and Fleet females just looking for fun.

But he wasn't cut off from what was happening three hundred kilometers away as the Sergeant Major was sending him nightly updates. And based on what Malachi was seeing from the reports, the Battalion was giving as good or better than they received considering the Lancers opposing his troops were all Centaurian which meant they were as good as they came in the field.

At the end of the two weeks, Malachi was standing behind his staff as the Marine Sector Commander stood before the gathered Staff and Company officers with the report of the observers in his hands.

"Ladies, Gentlemen, when I first heard of Colonel Thoris' idea of removing himself from the war games, I thought it was a foolish and insane. I have to say I was wrong. I have in my hand one of the best After-Action Reports I have ever seen for a newly formed Battalion, and the Lancers tell me they are very impressed and we both know they do not give out praise unless it is earned. Congratulations Marines of the Twelfth Battalion, you are hereby certified ready for deployment."

The General left with his staff and Malachi's staff turned back to him waiting to see what he had to say.

"People stand the Battalion down until tomorrow morning then we are going to pack up and head back to the luxury of the barracks. The perimeter will stay as it is for future units to train in, so all we need to do is make sure it is clean of trash and our gear. Trucks will here tomorrow afternoon by sixteen hundred to carry the Battalion back to the base. Once all the equipment is cleaned and accounted for, the Battalion will take a two week shore leave before we get back down to business."

He stood looking at the Officers then smiled.

"Outstanding job people. Now we're burning daylight, let's get this show on the road!"

The officers scattered to start the ball rolling with Major Prescott, the Exec walking up to Malachi and offering his hand.

"Thanks Colonel, I messed up several times but learned from those mistakes. I thought running a Company was rough, then the job as Battalion Exec is no pleasure cruise, but a Battalion Commander is rougher than I thought. Thanks for the lesson."

Malachi still had ahold of Prescott's hand and put his other hand on his shoulder.

"Walt, if I didn't think you could handle it, I wouldn't have enjoyed the two weeks fishing. We both learned something and on my side is that I really don't care for fishing that much."

Prescott laughed then they headed for the Command Bunker.

Deployment

When the Sector Commander gave his report on the war games, Malachi had two things in his jacket pocket. First was a copy of the report and second orders for the Battalion to lift, deploy aboard the Marine Assault Transport Fitzsimmons for a nine to twelve month tour, depending upon political conditions within the sector.

The Fitzsimmons had just gone through a complete refit and had an entirely new crew. For the first month of the cruise, Malachi fended off several women until they gave up and moved on to other men.

They were on the return route to Keres when Sergeant Major Beckett sat in his office sipping on coffee and brought up Malachi's celibacy.

"Colonel, it has been noticed by the Battalion that you have become a monk in reference to off duty time. Something wrong Sir?"

"Sergeant Major no, nothing wrong, I'm just not interested."

"Pardon my asking, is there someone special back on Keres then?"

Malachi leaned back in his chair and stared at the ceiling for a moment before answering.

"At one time there was, but as it is in our line of work they are no longer on Keres and to be honest, I'm not sure if they were that special. No that came out wrong. I think we were two ships passing in space and joined for a time, but that was before Ramstein and we both know how that turned out. She's probably got someone tending to her needs now and I've matured to the point that sex is not the end all of enjoyment."

"Pardon me Colonel, we are close to the same age and I'll be damned if I'm going to agree with that statement."

Malachi laughed knowing the Sergeant Major was keeping company with a Sub-Lieutenant from Navigation who was young enough to be his daughter.

"You might be right Sergeant Major, but I'm good."

The only excitement the Battalion had during this cruise was deploying to the planet Hancock at the request of the opposing political party to ensure the elections were properly held. Malachi caused quite a stir when he announced two days before the election that each person presenting themselves to vote would dip their finger in a bright, yellow ink to show they voted and there would be no way to remove the ink except for it wearing off. This was to prevent an individual from voting at one polling place then going to another to vote again.

The Marines would also oversee the counting of ballots and the protection of them during transportation once more to ensure no voter fraud was possible. When the votes were tabulated, there were over one hundred thousand less votes than the previous election and the opposing party had a narrow victory. It did not take a master mathematician to realize that during the previous election the winning party won by almost the number of missing voters than this election.

Back on Keres, once again as soon as everything was put away, the Battalion went on three weeks shore leave. Malachi had five Marines who were to do extra punishment duty form minor offenses while on ship or shore, but he stood them tall and told them they could also take leave but they had to understand once leave was over, they would stand their punishment duty.

What he didn't tell them was if they were to stay back and do the duty, then someone had to stay back with them to supervise them meaning that person or persons would miss out on taking leave. The word quickly spread throughout the Battalion of what he had done and during the leave, not one individual got in trouble knowing they would have to face him while he was also on leave.

Malachi finally spent one night with a Lieutenant Commander from the Destros Base Logistics office during the last week of the leave and as refreshing as the night was, he never attempted to carry it any further than that one night. He was putting all of his energy into the Battalion and felt he still had time for romance. That is if he survived long enough which was another reason he pulled back from engaging with females. He found he was actually afraid of becoming attached to one and them suffering his loss.

The experiences of Italia and Ramstein began to give him a jaundiced look at life in general.

Eight months back on Keres with training new people who replaced those who left the Battalion because of promotions or end of enlistments came to a halt when they boarded the Hermes for the planet Berkley to support the planet's militia in putting down a rebellion.

Berkley

One aspect of serving as a Marine was you often found yourself on what you would consider the wrong side of a fight, but even the Federation Throne had to accept that they would send people in on the wrong side simply because that side was the elected government. The purpose of the Marines was to quell a rebellion then allow the Federation Government sort out all of the details and in following the Principles of Leadership, deal with the problems at hand.

This was what Malachi found himself in the middle of in putting down this rebellion except he was facing nearly half of the former militia in doing so. He was also handicapped by the fact the government of Berkley was trying to mediate with the rebels and were not allowing any manner of air support for Malachi to draw upon.

The Hermes had landed out on the primary continent, off loaded the entire Battalion, then lifted taking the Marines Assault Boats with them. Malachi took advantage of having all of his ground transport vehicles available and had them loaded with ammunition and rations beyond what they actually needed including their heavy 120mm mortars and two basic loads of ammunition.

Malachi had a bad feeling from the drop of how things might turn out and was holding as much as he could in reserve, unexposed to either the opposition or the two Brigades he was supporting.

They had been pushing the rebels for nearly a month when Malachi got a bed feeling about the way the rebels were falling back and the fact the two Brigades were not keeping up with the Marines forward drive. In fact they almost seemed to be lying back, waiting for something to happen, and when they did engage, the fight seemed to stall them instead of pushing hard against the rebels.

Malachi was standing on top of his Command Car watching the rebels falling back with his people trying to maintain contact while the allied Brigades seemed stalled in place.

He called for his people to stop their advance and hold what they had. The Battalion was strung out in a manner that could be dangerous if suddenly pressed. Malachi looked back to the ridge they had crossed and thinking this open ground was bad news.

"Major Dunlap pull everyone in and back to that ridge where we can regroup. I don't like all this open ground without air support."

"Yes Sir!" Responded his Operations Officer.

Malachi looked over at his Intelligence officer.

"Captain Johannsen, are we still feeding our allies via the satellites?"

"Yes Sir, they can see everything we're doing."

"Kill the feed Captain, now."

"Yes Sir."

It was a tense two hours as the Battalion pulled back and onto the open ridge behind them. But this also gave the Battalion the high ground with the Berkley Brigades below them. Malachi had his people dig in, the ammunition being carried in the trucks off-loaded and spread out. His mortar crews dug in placing their 90mm mortars and 120's in a manner to use either one depending on the mission, or both at the same time if needed.

They were in the Command Bunker as it was being completed when Dunlap asked what Malachi was thinking pulling back as they had.

"Thomas, somewhere in my head is a memory of a Lancer Battalion getting suckered into an extended fight, spread out then the friendly units they were linked up with turned on them, joined the other side. Something about this fight does not seem right.

The rebels are giving ground against us when if they dug in would stop us cold since our allies are doing very little to support the operation."

"Colonel, I've noticed they have been very quiet about us pulling back. If I was commanding one of those brigades, I'd be wanting to know what the hell you were doing."

"I noticed that too. Captain Pettigrew, has all of the ordinance and field rations been distributed to the positions?"

"Yes Sir, as per your orders."

"Thank you. Thomas, consider this. The Rebels have light armor as does the Sixth Brigade to our right, yet neither has fielded that armor. The Fifth to our left has no armor so let's move half of the anti-armor weapons to our right to cover that area a bit better."

"You think they are going to turn on us?"

"I'm not going to take any chances. Lieutenant Laca, connect me with the Hermes please."

"Yes Sir." His Communications officer responded.

Seconds later the response came from the Hermes.

"Gander Six this is Hermes Actual, what's going on down there? We just observed you falling back uncontested. Over."

"Hermes, this is Six, this just feels bad. Any word from the capital concerning talks with the rebel leaders, over."

"Negative Six."

"Okay Hermes keep a close eye on things for us. We're going to sit here until something breaks, Gander Six out."

"Will do. Hermes out."

The worse part of waiting for something to happen is the waiting itself. The only good part was the troops had the chance to rest after being on the go for so long once they completed their positions. But even as some were resting, others were moving out front of their positions setting up intrusion devices to warn them in case of satellite failure which they had trained to do during their time in the field on Keres.

The first devices were set out at roughly five hundred meters then a second set at three hundred meters. Once set up, everyone took a deep breath and tried to relax. The Marines knew something was up otherwise the Colonel would not have pulled them back into such a defensive position and broke out the heavy mortars and anti-armor weapons.

The Sergeant Major made a tour of the positions and told the people the Colonel was just being cautious since the friendlies were not pulling their share of the load.

Lieutenant Laca was busy fielding calls from the people they were supporting asking why they had pulled back and why the Intelligence feeds had stopped. She just responded to them that the Battalion was worn down and needing to rest before further pursuing the rebels. Laca also told them the command module which transmitted the satellite data to them had been damaged by a stray bullet and was being repaired, once repairs were done, they would reestablish the links.

Malachi just smiled at Laca's soothing tones and how easy she lied about what they were doing. But it was also during this time that events above the planet began to worry Malachi along with the Captain of the Hermes.

The Frigate Benwin, who was their escort, received a call to respond to a Transport Freighter in distress and had to break orbit, leaving the Hermes with only their own guns to protect themselves. The Captain of the Benwin sent four sections, two platoons of their Marines, along with their Armored Assault Boats to the Hermes to stand by if needed on the ground. Once on board the Hermes, the boats were loaded to capacity with ammunition and rations in case those were also needed on the ground.

Water is always a problem as a person can go days without food, but water is essential on a daily basis. As the Marine Engineers were digging trenches to connect the bunkers the

Infantry were constructing, a team was utilizing their high speed drilling rig in search for water based upon a Geological satellite survey of the ridge. It took eight hours of drilling before they hit water and begin filling their collapsible tanks and every container available. They then encircled the well and water tanks with their trucks and equipment to protect that source from ground fire and to provide for their own fighting positions.

Malachi toured the perimeter the next morning talking to the men and women making sure they all knew what he was feeling. He told them to rest and hopefully the planets government would get off their asses and connect with the rebels and stop the war.

Towards late afternoon, it was noticed that the half dozen armored vehicles the Sixth Brigade had were moving, shifting positions as were the five tanks the Rebels had available. Also it looked as if companies in both the attached Brigades were shifting positions and from the looks of it, they were shifting towards the Marines.

Malachi instructed his Company Commanders that if the shooting starts, their mortars were to focus on that armor first. The Marines 120mm mortars had seeker heads plus armor penetration capabilities. If they laid enough of the 120's in on the armor, some should get through any anti-mortar protection and remove that threat. From then on, let the spotters control the mortar fire.

He had just released his commander's back to their company's when a call came in from Hermes.

Gander, this is Hermes, over."

"Go ahead Hermes, this is Gander, over."

"Gander, our sensors show three possibly light destroyers firing up their engines at the Berkley space port over."

"Hermes, your opinion over?"

"Gander it might get real busy up here all things considered, over."

"Recommendations, over?"

"Gander, we are going to drop the platoons from Benwin to you at dusk if possible, as I'm launching everything we have that can fight including the Assault Boats to give us as much protection as possible, but if it drops in the pot on the ground, you're on your own until we can get control of the situation up here if possible, over."

"Hermes, this is Gander Six, understand and good luck, over."

"Gander Six, this is Hermes Actual, I think we are both going to need a lot of luck this night. May the Saints watch over you. Hermes out."

As the Assault Boats were landing, the rebels began launching surface to surface rockets at the perimeter. The first rockets landed short but the Marines knew they would soon get their range.

Malachi sent one platoon into the trenches to face the Brigade to their left and the other to face the Brigade to their right. He came up on the all Battalion communications frequency to issue his final orders to his people.

"Marines, we can tangle with the rebels at any time but we must allow the people on our flanks to start the fight. They must fire the first shots at us before we can reply. All personnel go to purple and be ready for what may come. May the Saints watch over us this night."

Purple was nothing more than a set of patches each Marine would wear on their uniform which could only be seen via the Marine's helmets night vision. It was worn on both shoulders and the chest and back. The purpose was if they got overran during the night, any person seen without such patches was a target.

As the first rockets were finding the range, the Marine's 120's began firing. Those watching the rebel advances noted the large explosions soon after the 120's opened up with the rocket trucks being hit along with their armor.

"Gander, this is Hermes, we are under attack, over."

"Good luck Hermes. So are we. Gander out."

Suddenly the Marines lost all satellite feeds as it was apparent with the Hermes under attack, those vessels also knocked out the satellites covering them.

It was in full darkness that the armor of the Sixth Brigade opened fire on the Marines as they advanced towards the perimeter. Malachi thought how foolish the commanders were attacking his dug in positions at that time. In an hour the moon would be up and it was full this coming night, giving his Marines more advantage over the equipment the rebels were using. Yes, at this time, the Brigades he had been supporting were now rebels.

Malachi sent his staff out to their own bunkers leaving only himself, Major Dunlap his Operations Officer and Lieutenant Laca along with her radio operators in the Command Bunker. The Sergeant Major had taken Malachi's shadows, his driver, clerk, runner, and radio operator out during the day and had them dig in at the entrance of the Command Bunker to protect it from infiltrators.

Charlie Company's Commander had his 120's fire Illumination at maximum range but timed not to light up the battle ground, but to burn out on the ground. The grass was at the stage of turning brown for the autumn and it quickly caught fire. This back lighted the rebels without interfering with the Marines night vision.

Alpha Company pounded the Sixth Brigade with their 120's and taking a cue from Charlie Company, also dropped Illumination rounds onto the ground, but in the middle of the Sixth Brigade, breaking up their formations.

The Fifth Brigade was advancing on the Marines but had yet to fire a shot as they moved forward. But since they were not being fired upon, they were the first to break the sensor line at five hundred meters from the perimeter and set off the attached flares. The men in front that had broken the sensor line opened fire with small arms only to be met with the raking fire of the Marine's Heavy weapons.

Soon nearly two-thirds of the perimeter was under fire with the Marines taking their time, picking their targets and removing the threat as the rebels pressed forward.

The mortars fired the last of the 120 ammunition at it's minimum range then switched to the 90mm mortars and began focusing on large groups in front of the positions. Sniping began to hit the part of the perimeter which was not under direct attack, but the Marines just waited until a second shot from that location then pounded it with their Heavy Weapons.

Malachi order half of Bravo's Mortars to swing around and support the defense of Alpha and Charley Companies. But it was not slowing down the advances of the rebels as they hit the three hundred meter sensors and flares.

Soon a call was heard: "Here they come!"

The rebels rushed the perimeter in mass in hopes of overrunning the Marines and crushing them. Those that made it inside the perimeter, jumping over the trenches soon found themselves fighting against the Engineers, Cooks, and clerks with no where to run. Those that dropped into the trenches faced Marines who had trained for such fighting and never gave them any quarter, stacking up bodies in the trenches till some parts almost became impassable.

Malachi could only stand in the Command Bunker listening to the fighting outside and thinking he should be out there with his men, but the one time he started to the bunker exit, the Sergeant Major put his hand on Malachi's chest to hold him back.

"You're job is in here to coordinate if necessary, not out there to get your ass blown away. I'll go see what needs to be done and deal with it."

Neither man spoke as the Sergeant Major left the bunker at a run.

The fighting raged for hours with those inside the perimeter slowly filling in the gaps on the perimeter as directed by their commanders. All Malachi could do was listen and pray it would soon let up as it seemed there was one long call for Corpsmen to attend to the wounded.

It was three in the morning, over six hours after the first shots were fired that a sudden silence fell over the ridge. Malachi walked to the exit to the bunker and found two of his people dead, his driver and his runner, with another wounded in fighting that came close to the bunker entrance. In their places was a Cook and an Engineer.

He stepped further out and looked towards the Engineer equipment and saw how it was broken with one vehicle burning as a couple of Engineers were attempting to put the fire out.

Malachi was lost in the image being presented to him via his night vision. The interior of the perimeter was littered with bodies of both rebels and Marines from the patches he could see. He turned back and entered the bunker. Malachi may not have been in the fight, but he was broken as bad as his command.

Lieutenant Laca had her helmet off and a headset on as she rested her head on the table her console was sitting on. It was silent for a long time in the bunker until the speakers crackled.

"Marines, this is Lieutenant Rostenkowski of the Sixth Brigade, I request a cease fire and await your terms, over."

Laca looked over at Malachi who motioned for her to respond.

"Sixth Brigade, this is Gander, lay down all arms and return to the positions you held before you attacked. We'll discuss terms after daylight. Over."

"Understand Gander, and will comply."

Laca looked at Malachi.

"A lieutenant?"

"Could be he is the ranking officer. And you made the right call Captain Laca. As soon as I can, I'll cover the paperwork."

"Thank you Sir."

Malachi sat waiting for his staff to return since the shooting had stopped but no one returned, not even the Sergeant Major. This worried him but there was a lot of work outside that needed dealt with and it was possible they were busy getting things lined out. Laca's senior operator brought Malachi a cup of strong coffee and left him alone. Major Dunlap was busy with his Operations Sergeant as they were getting reports in from the Company's concerning casualties and unit status. He had let Major Dunlap run the battle during the night unless Dunlap asked him for his advice.

Malachi was standing at the exit to the bunker when the sun came up and in the faint daylight, the carnage looked even worse. Marines were moving from body to body, removing any weapons from the Rebels and checking their own to see if life was still present. Calls for Corpsmen could still be heard within the perimeter as he just walked out into the area. He looked behind him to see a Marine sitting on an ammunition crate with their head in their hands. It wasn't until he got close he realized it was Captain Wolenski, and the body lying near the crate was Captain Pettigrew. He knew that the two of them had gotten close since the field exercises and now Pettigrew was dead.

"Alicia, are you going to be okay?" He asked his Adjutant?"

She looked up at him, her face shield open and tears flowing down her cheeks.

"Yes Sir, I'll be alright. Stephen was moving to provide support when he was killed. I was right behind him with four clerks heading for the perimeter when he went down. He was dead when I got to him so I continued with my mission. Colonel, now I know why you will not sleep with a member of your command."

"Alicia, go to the Command Bunker and grab a cup of coffee. It's not doing you any good sitting out here with him."

"Yes Sir." She stood, looked back down at the broken body of her lover then slowly walked off towards the bunker.

Malachi watched her walk away, then moved out to the perimeter where the original rebels struck it. He stepped up on a bunker and just looked out at the sea of bodies before him. He was soon joined by another Marine. It was Captain Johannsen his Intelligence officer and his left arm was in a sling.

"Colonel, we lost Major Prescott and the Sergeant Major Sir. Both bodies are in the Aid Station. Sir why did they just keep coming at us like that?"

"I don't know James, but I will find out. Get to the Command Bunker and see if they can raise the Hermes. We need to get as many of our wounded aboard ship as quickly as possible if it is even possible."

As Malachi began walking around the perimeter, he noticed that the Marines killed during the night had been removed from the bunkers and trenches and covered with their ponchos. Those Marines that saw him only nodded and went back to what they were doing in case there were still people out there wanting to fight them.

Malachi never tried to count the number of dead he had to deal with as his mind was still trying to work out the reason why the rebels pushed the attack as they were being cut down like wheat.

"Gander Six, stand by for patch to Hermes, over."

"Standing by."

"Gander Six this is Hermes Actual. What is your status over?"

"My Battalion is beat to hell but intact. What is your status over?"

"Same here Six, but we lost a lot of good people."

"Same here Hermes. How soon can you send a shuttle, or Assault Boat to move our wounded up to you over?"

"It'll be several more hours Six, but I can send down some medical support and supplies. Over."

"Please do and if you have a spare Assault Boat. Send it as I want something here with some more firepower in case this fight is not over yet. Over."

"Will do Six, Hermes out."

Malachi could see rebels carrying white flags moving amongst the bodies looking for wounded. He also noticed if they touched a firearm, they just tossed it aside so they could tend to any individual still alive.

When he walked back into the Command Bunker, what was left of his staff were just sitting, waiting for the next boot to drop. Major Dunlap handed him a note with the rough figures of dead and wounded. Even with the reinforcements, he had lost over a third of his Battalion. Ninety-seven confirmed dead was the worst part of it all for him.

"Major Dunlap, please locate the senior member of the Engineers and if they have any equipment or energy left, we need to start burying our dead."

"Yes, Sir. I'll go do that now."

Dunlap left the Bunker and Malachi just sat down and leaned back against the sandbagged wall of the bunker. Within minutes he was asleep.

It was nearly three hours before Alicia Wolenski woke him with a cup of hot coffee.

"Colonel, the Engineers are digging the graves and Chief Lambert is collecting the information of each individual along with the data packs from their helmets. The Hermes contacted us about five minutes ago and will start sending down what transportation they have left. Besides the Assault Boat we have down here, they have three left up stairs and only one shuttle. From what we understand, the rebels sent eight ships up after the Hermes and it was a street fight. Hermes lost six of their fighters in the fight, and the Assault Boats they lost were from being launched to provide what support they could provide. Colonel, this is one for the books."

"Yes, but which side of the story will we come out on?"

Alicia leaned over to him so she could whisper to him.

"Colonel I heard what the Sergeant Major told you before he left the bunker. He was right, your place was in here to coordinate the defense, not out there to get yourself killed, so how about you put the guilt of being alive aside and start thinking about getting us out of this shithole, Sir."

"What's the word on the rebels?"

"It's over. Everyone has pulled back and are licking their wounds Sir. One of the officers from the Sixth came into the perimeter. Captain Johannsen spoke with him. According to James, the rebels were told once it got hot for us, we'd call for a cease fire, but once the attack started, it got out of control and when they realized we were not going to stand down, it was too late to stop the attack."

"Foolish people."

"Yes Sir."

It would be four more days before the first of the remaining personnel of the Battalion were lifted off the planet after all of the wounded was removed. Before the first man was lifted, a service for the dead was held over the graves on top of the ridge.

Once aboard the Hermes, it was not hard to see the damage they took as some walls were smoked and some even had paint peeling from fires inside the ship. The Hermes had suffered twenty-eight dead and sixty-three wounded. Wounded sailors and Marines lined the halls as there was not enough room in the

Medical Bay for all of them. Malachi went from Marine to Marine checking on each individual before going to his own quarters to start his After-Action Report based upon the fractional reports from his staff and Company's.

Returning

It took the Hermes two additional weeks to return to Keres because of the battle damage to its engines. Each day Malachi walked the passageways of the ship, visiting with the wounded and any Marine he met. As badly as the Battalion was beat up, every Marine thanked him for the training he pushed them through, telling him it was those long days in the field that held them together, gave them the confidence to do what had to be done.

A week out of Keres, Captain Laca knocked on his quarters door, and when he opened it, she just moved into his room without speaking. He looked at her as she began removing her uniform. Michele Laca was not the best looking woman he had ever been with but it wasn't the physical appearance that was important even to Malachi. She was half way undressed before she finally spoke.

"We both know that one of us will be transferred once the dust settles after Berkley, and we both need this."

She would come to him nightly for the next week and each night was full of passion and desire until she proclaimed she was finally sedated and she thanked him for the time.

Malachi sat in his quarters the night before entering orbit around Keres and thought that Laca was right, he needed the feeling of another human being at night to relax and once more regain control of his thoughts and feelings.

The Hermes was damaged to the point they could not make a landing at Destros, but had to transfer all personnel to the surface via shuttles with the wounded dropping first then the Battalion. Once all unnecessary personnel were off the ship, it moved into a space dock for initial repairs to begin.

Malachi was the last individual of the Battalion to leave the ship. When he stepped off the shuttle ramp, he was facing the Sector Commander, General Rawleigh and his staff. Malachi felt uneasy seeing the General but walked up to him and saluted.

"General Rawleigh, are you here to relieve me Sir?"

"No Colonel but we have a lot to discuss about what happened on Berkley."

"Sir, am I under arrest?"

"Of course not Colonel, why would you ask that?"

"Sir, if I have not been relieved of command and not under arrest, I would politely ask that I tend to my Battalion first Sir. I want to make sure they are settling in and being taken care of Sir."

"Of course Colonel. In fact we can do what we have planned at your headquarters. If you'll join us in my vehicle, we'll get going and let you tend to the business of your command."

"Thank you General."

At Battalion Headquarters, Malachi turned the care of the General and his staff over to Captain Wolenski, then went to the barracks to check on his people. Each section were cleaning out the lockers of those killed to make them available for replacements at the same time insuring that all personal belongings were ready to ship to their next of kin after making sure nothing embarrassing was included.

Of those personnel in the hospital, only those who lost limbs were being packed up for later disposition. He checked the kitchens to see if they needed anything before heading back to his offices and the questions awaiting him. He walked into the conference room to deal with the questions he was unsure if he wanted to hear much less answer.

"Colonel Thoris, I've asked Captain Wolenski to remain in the room and record all questions and comments. This is not an investigation into the events on Berkley, only questions to clarify a few points that we feel are unclear in your After Action Report." General Rawleigh commented.

"Alright General." Malachi responded.

"First, why did you pull back to what is now being called Thoris' Ridge?"

"I can think of better names for that ridge General, especially since we buried too many good men and women on that ridge. But to answer your question Sir, I became concerned that our so called allies were not only not picking up their fair share, they were forcing us into a situation out on that open plain of being caught between them and the rebels. I remembered a story of a Lancer Battalion getting caught in a like situation about twenty years ago. Their allies turned on them and joined the rebels. If memory serves me right, we came out just a few percentage points better than the Lancers because of my actions."

"Colonel Thoris, we view that as a sound, tactical move, it was just that we could not get a good feeling of why in the middle of an advance you'd turn around and return to terrain you had already covered."

"General, that ridge gave us the tactical advantage in that we had even greater fields of fire than if we had stayed down on the flats. We had the high ground which was another thing that was bothering me. The rebels gave up that ridge with barely a fight. If they had dug in their armor, we'd have never been able to push them off that ridge without air support and that was taken away from us at the start of the operation."

"Yes, Colonel, we have discussed that mistake with the diplomatic people in depth. Never again will Marines or Lancers sent down without their air support. What else?"

"I, actually we, being my staff figured the rebels were not exposing their armor because the Sixth Brigade also had armor. In retrospect, I should have targeted the rebels armor early in the engagement just to remove the threat, but since it stayed off the battlefield, I ignored it. They did not even use it as artillery, which confused me."

Malachi took a drink of the hot tea which Wolenski had set in front of him before continuing.

"General there were so many things just wrong with how the rebels were falling back coupled with our allies also holding back. We had taken casualities, but the rebels could or should have been making us pay a higher price for the ground they gave up. I was seriously worried we were being suckered into a kill sack of our own making. So I pulled back and we dug in Sir."

"Colonel Thoris, from what we have read concerning the time line, I think it is very possible by your pulling back, you may have put the rebels off their own time line and that gave you the time to dig in and get ready for them."

"General, yes, I think you are correct Sir. If they had hit us out on the flats, in the middle of that plain, we would have had to fight while digging in and under those circumstances it is very likely I would not be sitting here today, nor any of my people returning to tell the tale."

The questions and answers carried on until time for the evening meal before the General decided he had heard enough.

"Lieutenant Colonel Thoris, you did a superb job building the Twelfth and in developing a solid defense against what can only be considered in the neighborhood of eighteen to one odds on Berkley. We'll start arranging for replacements for your killed and wounded when we return to Sector Headquarters so you can reform the Battalion."

"Excuse me General, do not send me any personnel to replace my wounded until the Medical personnel determines that an individual is no longer fit for service. Sir, I promised my people they would have a place within the Twelfth once free of the hospital. I invite the General to go to Destros and talk to those men and women in the hospital and see what they desire. I think you will find even those missing limbs wish to return to the Twelfth."

"Colonel Thoris, I'll instruct the Sector Adjutant to only fill the slots of those killed in action and await for a call of needed personnel once they have time to heal up and be evaluated for duty status. In giving this some consideration, I suspect you will have some promotions into empty slots you wish to deal with at this level?"

"Correct Sir, and I wish to thank the General and his Staff for the speedy approval of the field promotion of Captain Laca. I'll try to have a solid list to Sector within the week Sir."

General Rawleigh stood and offered his hand to Malachi.

"Malachi, I think my predecessor made the right choice in giving you the Twelfth. But be warned, I'll give you two years to rebuild the Twelfth considering the time it will take for a lot of your people to escape the hospital, then I see even bigger things in your future. As of right now, the Twelfth is on thirty days recreational leave here on Keres. From what I have heard, you'll probably be working through it but do try to put your boots up and relax, you've earned it."

"Thank you Sir, but if you do not mind, we'll start leave in three days. We still have to process the personal belongings of those who did not return with us.."

"Yes, of course. Fair evening Colonel."

"Fair evening General."

He sat for a long time thinking he had dodged a bullet since his command was shot all to hell. He looked over at Captain Wolenski who was still sitting against the wall.

"Alicia, we have a lot of work and only three days to do it. Can we do it?"

"It'll be done in two days since I started on it while in transit. Colonel, you have worried yourself over this until it has almost made you sick. But if I may be so bold, I think the time you spent with Michele has eased your stress factor immensely."

He looked at Alicia, then smiled.

"There are no secrets aboard a ship are there?"

"No Sir, there isn't?"

"Now if I may be so bold. How are you doing?"

106

"Sir, it's been almost two months since Stephen was killed, but I'm fine Sir. They say that nothing in the Fleet is guaranteed, but within the Marines, separation is pretty much a given. We were lovers, but never to the point we were planning a flower garden together in our old age. I'm alright Sir, thank you for asking."

She got up to leave when Malachi spoke again before she got to the door.

"Alicia, once the dust settles, would you consider dinner with me?"

"I'll think about it."

He just nodded and she left the room. He sat for a short time then got up, deciding that he had wasted enough time already.

On Lake Pilar, there were several small islands, the remains of hill tops that would never be covered with water as the lake filled to capacity. On those islands cabins were built for use by Fleet personnel insuring them privacy during their stay. Malachi and Alicia stayed on one of those islands for three weeks with him working on promotions and reassignments within the Battalion when they were not making love.

He would often sit out on the veranda looking out over the water as Alicia lay nude on the deck, sunbathing. As she had told him when she finally accepted his invitation to dine together, the General made it clear he would get the Battalion back in working order, but he'd never take it into battle again.

He moved Major Dunlap into the Executive Officers slot, then moved Captain Johannsen into the Operations Officer slot with a promotion to Major. Alicia's field was Administration and he could only leave her in that slot and keep her as a Captain. She told him the only way she could receive a promotion was to transfer to a higher organization into a Major's slot and she was happy where she was at, meaning she really doubted that Marine Headquarters would allow her to stay until the two years were up.

Rebuilding

Only one First Sergeant survived Berkley but spent six months in the hospital recovering from wounds. Malachi had him promoted to Sergeant Major once he passed the physical and reported for duty. His name was Carrington and after Berkley, he carried a fire deep inside to make sure the Twelfth was ready, even better than before. Malachi had to lightly counsel him to slow down a bit, but still let him keep a fire under the Battalions Non-Commissioned Officers.

Only seventy-two percent of the personnel hospitalized were able to return to duty due to the extent of their wounds. Malachi, Dunlap and Wolenski worked long hours shuffling people around and promoting those needing promoting to fill in the ranks with new people reporting in. Some of those with non-Infantry specialties were brought in to fill higher ranking positions than Malachi could justify promoting people into.

By the end of the first year, the Battalion was back up to full strength. This also brought about the transfer of Alicia Wolenski to Sector Headquarters into the assignment as the Regimental Adjutant of the Third Marine Regiment.

Both of them had been celibate since Lake Pilar, but he spent another week with her on the lake before she lifted off Keres. Her replacement was a male Senior Lieutenant which actually made Malachi happy in that he did not have another female to deal with. His relationship with Michele Laca had ended before arriving on Keres and she had found herself a Fleet Senior Lieutenant assigned to Destros Base to keep time with.

As when he first built the Twelfth, he took them to the field but this time for only six months since nearly seventy percent of his people had already experienced the training and they fired up the rest. His Senior Sergeants kept the new officers wired up and in line as they often explained what was happening and how to deal with things that Malachi was throwing at them in getting them ready as it was a change from what they were used too.

The Battalion was certified in twenty-one months, three months ahead of the twenty-four which Malachi had been given. With the certification, Malachi was handed orders. He had orders to Tantus as the Executive Officer of the Third Regiment. This put him back in proximity of Alicia Wolenski since being the Regimental Exec and her being the Regimental Adjutant, he was once again her boss.

When Malachi stepped off the shuttle on Tantus, he found Alicia waiting on him with a ground car. Even before he was close enough to speak to her, she raised her left hand to show a ring on it. He smiled as he closed the distance between them.

"Congratulations Alicia."

"Thank you Mal, but you're the blame for this?"

"I am? How so?"

"I have been fighting off Gerald's, my husband's proposals for months until I received a copy of your orders. Malachi, I have always had strong feelings for you but I can honestly say I love Gerald, so I accepted his proposal and we married a week later. By doing so I removed any temptation I might have to rekindle our relationship."

"Alicia, I do hope you have a wonderful life with this man. We both know my life is about as screwed up as humanly possible and you deserve stability."

They talked about the Regiment on the way to their Headquarters where he signed in then met with the Regimental Commander.

Malachi took on the assignment as he always did and that was total and complete. One of his functions was to insure the Battalion's were ready to fight and they had what they needed to fight with. Since his function was logistics of the Regiment, he avoided any tactical discussion whenever possible, but he might be found standing in a field kitchen during field exercises checking on how well the personnel were being fed. He was never overly critical and rarely wrote a report critical of what he found.

It did take over six months before this hero wearing two Medal's of Valor was recognized as just a Marine who worked hard at his job and had found himself in bad situations requiring tough decisions.

He would spend four years as Regimental Exec before he received orders back to Keres as the Regimental Commander of the Fifth Regiment at the rank of full Colonel. And as when on Tantus, he kept his personal relationships far apart until he reported to Keres with a year since his last physical engagement with a female.

Being on Keres where the Federation Throne was located and being the Commander of the largest Marine unit on the planet, he often found himself at the Palace either in discussions with the Prince, or at formal parties.

Before the first party, the Prince warned him that he could find himself with a lot of attention since he was well known within the Federation. Malachi found himself being propositioned by several ladies during the first party, including the wife of an Ambassador desiring his sexual company. Malachi was polite and went back to his quarters alone.

It was at the third party he attended that he met the Captain of the Prince's personal ship, a Centaurian with coal black fur. That night started a two year relationship between them spending as much time together as duty would allow without committing to anything further than just enjoy the time together.

When she transferred to Fleet Headquarters on Denoyelles, Malachi just moved on with his life with a night here and there stretching over months as he just attended to his Regiment with Battalions being deployed as needed.

Twice he lifted with the Prince as they toured several worlds with Malachi's purpose being in looking at places for Marine Outposts if needed along the expanding Rim of the Federation.

At the end of his four year tour of duty, Malachi was once more given a new assignment. He was going to Denoyelles to assume command of the Federation Marine's Officer Candidate School also known as the Cadet Course. Malachi considered it just another way of the Marine Headquarters to keep him in service yet out of harm's way, but he lifted from Keres determined to do a good job and present the Fleet with solid Marine officers.

Denoyelles

Malachi stepped out of his ground vehicle which picked him up at the Space Port and looked at the gate to the Marine Officer School and the buildings beyond. It had dawned on him he had left those very same gates almost twenty-four years earlier and wondered where the time had gone.

He had been eighteen when he entered the Cadet Course after enlisting then being found to have a high IQ and given the chance to be an officer instead of an enlisted Marine. Of the one hundred in his Basic Course, he graduated fifth in his class. Now he was back as the School Commandant and it was his responsibility to provide the Marine units with qualified officers.

Malachi soon learned the school was between classes with a new class being gathered and scheduled to start within a month. He just threw himself in studying the course syllabus as he learned the names of his staff and instructors.

He remembered one thing about his time at the school and that was the Commandant rarely interacted with the students, leaving all contact to the instructors. As Commandant, he only interacted with a Cadet in extreme cases of disciplinary action if needed, then again at graduation, commissioning the new Sub-Lieutenants.

The one thing he did like about this assignment was even though he was almost right next door to Federation Marine Headquarters, he was not subject to them requiring daily or weekly reporting on the actions within the school. Granted Headquarters had to approve all changes to the course syllabus, or any special requirement above normal operational funding.

It was nearly two weeks into training the new class that Malachi found himself having to counsel one of the female students as she had bounced one of her male students off a wall when he laid hands on her in the communal showers. When her file was laid on his desk the name on it gave him pause.

Her name was Belinda Thoris.

He read the file and just laid it aside as he could not believe what he had read. Her mother was Centaurian, a Lancer officer by the name of Emmanuel Braxton. She was twenty years old and had just finished the university on Hanover on a Lancer scholarship. Her date of acceptance into the Marines was two months before he was named as the new Commandant of the school.

Malachi left his office and went to the school's Medical officer and had him pull Cadet Thoris' DNA profile then had him compare it to his own profile. It came back as father and daughter. Malachi asked the Commander to keep this under his hat as it would not do Cadet Thoris any good if the word got out he was her father. The Commander agreed.

He returned to his office then contacted the classes training officer and had Cadet Thoris report to him.

When she entered and took the position of attention in the center of his desk, he could only see her mother at a young age except unless she had gone through the denuding process, there was no sign of her being a Centaurian. She was not looking at him but at a point above his head as she stood there, waiting for him to speak.

"Cadet Thoris, can you explain to me why Cadet Crossley is in Medical as the results of your actions?"

"Sir, I accept that interactions between the sexes is permissible, but it also requires the permission of the female if the male wishes to engage in sexual congress with the male. I had told Cadet Crossley three times since reporting that I had no desire to engage with him in such a manner Sir."

"Did you express yourself in such a manner before you bounced him off the shower facility's wall?"

"Yes Sir I did then he reached between my legs from behind Sir. Sir with all due respect to protocol, no individual except for physicians have touched me there and I was not going to allow him too. I am sorry that he was injured as he was Sir."

"Cadet, your records show you to be half Centaurian, do you fellow Cadets know this?"

"No Sir, they do not. My mother suggested that since I have no fur, not to advertise that part of my birth right Sir."

"As I understand it, you could have gone into the Lancers instead of the Marines. Would you care to tell me why you picked the Marines?"

She just stood quietly, not answering his question. Malachi stood up and leaned over his desk until he was eyeball to eyeball with her.

"Answer my question Cadet."

"Sir since my records are on your desk and you know I'm half Centaurian, then you should know that answer Sir."

Malachi stood upright, then walked to his door and closed it. He stepped back to her, took her by the shoulders and turned her around to look at him. He could feel her shaking as he held her.

"Belinda, who am I to you?"

She had tears in her eyes as she answered.

"You're my father Sir."

He pulled her to him and held her as tears filled his own eyes. He spoke to her as she shivered in his arms.

"Belinda, I never knew I had a daughter. I never knew."

"I know father, I know that mother never informed you of my birth."

"How is your mother? Did she remarry?"

"Mother is fine, she is still on Hanover and no Sir, she never remarried."

He pulled her head back and kissed her on her forehead before releasing her. He then walked back around his desk and sat down as she turned back to face him.

"Belinda, the name Thoris is not a common name but we cannot allow the other Cadets to know our relationship as it will not do you any good during this course. As Commandant, I must be impartial when dealing discipline and as much as it might bother me, I shall give you discipline for your actions."

"I have no problem in defending yourself, your honor or your person in the situation which you found yourself in, but you will have to control yourself in doing so. We are lucky that Cadet Crossley will only miss three days of training which he can make up, but it could have been more serious. I doubt anyone else will become so aggressive and I will speak to your trainers so they can also further explain about keeping ones hands to themselves."

"Yes Sir."

"Cadet Belinda Thoris, you will stand one hour a day of punishment duty for one week for using excessive force in dealing with Cadet Crossley. Do you accept your punishment Cadet?"

"Yes Sir, I accept Sir."

"Stand easy Cadet."

She relaxed her position.

"Belinda, the next time you contact your mother, please tell her…. Please tell her hello for me."

"I shall father, and may I say, that I am happy to have finally met you Sir. I've read every article, dispatch, story out there on you since I was old enough to read. Mother always spoke highly of you Sir."

"Belinda, I only wish I had watched you grow up and been a part of your life. But it did not happen and I was not aware your mother was pregnant the last time I saw her. Now if Lieutenant

115

Hammerly is in the outer office, send him in and remember what I said about letting people know about our relationship."

Belinda returned to the position of attention.

"Yes Sir, by your leave Sir."

"You're dismissed Cadet."

Malachi was filling out the disciplinary form on Belinda when her senior instructor entered his office taking a position such as she had. Malachi never looked up as he spoke.

"Lieutenant Hammerly, according to Cadet Thoris, Cadet Crossley laid hands on her after she had repeatedly told him she was not interested. I find no fault with Cadet Thoris' actions but I do find fault with her use of excessive force. She will spend one hour a day on punishment detail for one week."

"Yes Sir."

"Now Lieutenant, you will further reinforce the concept to the Cadets that no means no and any Cadet who wishes to ignore that concept will stand before me and they will remember that time for the rest of their career if they have one. I will not tolerate any female being used as a sex object. They are training to be Marine Officers and the communal shower facility is to get them used to the idea that we Marines, males and females must often be exposed to one another, the shower is not the entrance to a bordello. Make sure they understand what I am saying because if this happens again with any female and let's add males being harassed by either sex, I will teach the entire class including instructors a lesson they would rather not learn. Am I clear on this Lieutenant?"

"Yes Sir. A question Sir?"

"Ask it."

"Is Cadet Thoris any relation to you Sir?"

Malachi looked at him for a moment before answering.

"Yes Lieutenant, she is. She is my daughter, but one I never knew I had until today. When she walked through my door, that was the first time I ever laid eyes on her. Now I have to ask for your word as an officer to keep that secret. She is to get no special privilege since she is my daughter and if I find out she is, I'll rake that officer or NCO across the coals. Am I clear on that Lieutenant?"

"Sir if anyone asks, I'll just say her having the same name as you is just a fluke, an oddity Sir."

"Thank you Lieutenant. One other thing, her mother is a Centaurian, a full blood Centaurian and a Lancer so she has training far above what the other Cadets may have been exposed to prior to being here. Watch her carefully and keep her in check as much as possible. Crossley is lucky she didn't cripple him. But keep her heritage quiet also."

"Yes Sir."

Malachi handed the Disciplinary Form over to the Lieutenant for him to deal with. Once her punishment detail was complete, he would sign off on the form and turn it in to Administration to become part of her training record.

After Hammerly left the officer, Malachi opened Belinda's file again and pulled her photo from it and looked at it. He then inserted it into his viewer, blew it up and made a copy for himself.

Within the file was Emma's contact information which he copied down but was unsure of contacting her. What he never told Belinda was Emma was never out of his heart, just set aside as he figured he'd never see her again. But if Emma had never married, what was her feelings for him?"

Belinda said she had read everything possible about him growing up but that was also the Centaurian way. It was important to the Centaurians that the lineage of a child be known to them.

Malachi put her file back together then placed it into his out basket for his clerk to retrieve at the end of the day. He then turned to look out his window to the parade grounds and saw

Belinda running to rejoin her section in training on the obstacle course. Hammerly came into view and he motioned to the Sergeants that were not directly involved with training but were observing. From the looks on the Sergeant's faces, Hammerly was laying down the law to them concerning conduct between Cadets.

The thought went through Malachi's mind of how could things get so fouled up at this stage of his life. He now had a daughter he never knew existed, in a situation which would not allow him to even pretend to act like a father, and in knowing about her, old feelings once again creeped into his heart.

Belinda had her mother's looks but with auburn hair instead of Emma's blond hair and fur. Duty required him to treat her no different than any other Cadet, yet he hated having to give her punishment for defending herself. But her punishment would hopefully teach her self-control. Malachi had to then laugh as it seemed she may have inherited his temper which got him into trouble his first weeks in the Cadet Course here on Denoyelles.

He turned back to his desk and pressed the intercom to contact his clerk.

"Corporal Wilemon, would you bring me the file on Cadet Crossley please."

"Aye Sir." Was the response.

A minute later Corporal Wilemon entered with the file in hand.

"I figured the Colonel would want to see it Sir."

"Thank you Corporal." Malachi spoke as he accepted the file.

Wilemon left with Belinda's file and other documents in the Out Basket.

Malachi studied Crossley's file closely. He was from Jorgensen, made modest grades at the university there and what made Malachi smile was Crossley majored in Political Science.

Crossley was at the Cadet Course on an appointment from the Jorgensen Ambassador to the Federation on Hanover. Malachi knew his type as he had dealt with people like him before. He would enter service, then once he completed the basic requirements for time and duty, would resign their commission and return to their home world to run for political office.

Crossley's family dealt in Import/Export on Jorgensen and the Intelligence Report showed them to be honest, hardworking people. Again this was not uncommon as people thought in that some children would rather find an easier path to walk then follow their parents. Also Cadet Crossley was the fourth of six children and the second male child of the family.

It did not matter that Belinda put Crossley in the hospital, what mattered was why she put him there. Crossley would have to stand before Malachi as Belinda did. But Malachi could almost hear Crossley's excuse for what happened to him.

Malachi realized he could not sit in judgement on Crossley unless Crossley accepted his own guilt in the incident. He left his office for Lieutenant Colonel Mifflin's office, the Deputy School Commandant, who also happened to be female. Other than briefings and a get to know you dinner, contact between them had been sparse which suited Malachi just fine.

He tapped on her doorframe.

"Colonel Mifflin, do you have a minute?"

"Colonel Thoris you're the boss here so I had best find a minute Sir."

Malachi just smiled and entered her office. He handed the file on Crossley to her before taking a seat in front of her desk.

"Doris, I have a problem which you may need to deal with for me. You are aware of Cadet Thoris putting Cadet Crossley in the hospital for being aggressive in the shower facility."

"Yes Sir, I am aware of it. I saw Cadet Thoris leave a few minutes ago. May I ask your judgement in her case?"

119

"Certainly. Based on her unsworn testimony, Crossley groped her in the shower. She says she had told him more than once to leave her alone and this time he grabbed something that did not belong to him. She reacted to his touch and he found himself in the hospital. I gave her a week's punishment detail for being overly aggressive in defending herself."

"That sounds reasonable, now I sense a catch in this situation. Care to enlighten me."

"If you read Crossley's file, I think you will see what I see or suspect that once out of the hospital, he'll claim innocence and try to deflect the blame on Thoris. If he does, I cannot in good conscious pass judgement on him."

"Well Colonel, when I saw her name on the class roster, I was wondering if there could be a relationship problem."

"You could say that Doris, I discovered today that I'm a father. Cadet Thoris is my daughter from a relationship a long time ago. May I suggest you also look at her file."

"Does she know you are her father?"

"Yes, her mother insured she knew who her father was. You see, her mother is a Centaurian and a Lancer officer. Now before I gave her punishment, I made sure she understood not to divulge our relationship as it could cause problems with her classmates."

"Before you said that last part, I was inclined to think she might be using your relationship to ease her way. But if she is part Centaurian and raised by a Lancer Officer, that young lady would as soon loose an arm before she made such an attempt."

"My thinking also. Now if Crossley admits to his part in this incident, I think two weeks punishment detail is correct and proper. If he denies his part then I think sending him to the Psych Docs before any decision can be made concerning his conduct."

"Sir, do I have to remind you what the punishment for a cadet lying is?"

"No, but as I said, read his file, then you'll see the problem which we will have if he does deny, and is found to have lied about his conduct."

Malachi just set as she read over Crossley's file. It only took her about five minutes to digest the contents before speaking to him again.

"Colonel, if he claims innocence, I agree we need to turn him over to the Docs to sort out the truth so we can clear any hint of collusion on your part."

"Doris, here in the offices, please call me Malachi or even Mal. I see no offense in doing that. Now once he is released from the hospital and we can guarantee he is not on any manner of pain medications we shall stand him before my desk with you and Lieutenant Hammerly in attendance along with the recorders on. The minute he claims innocence, I am going to excuse myself from the proceedings and turn them over to you to avoid conflict of interest. You will have to order him to the Docs. Do you see any problem with that procedure?"

"No Malachi, I do not. What if he admits to his guilt?"

"Then I sentence him to two weeks and ensure he understands he is to never lay a hand on a female Cadet again."

"You do know what will happen to him if the Docs cannot clear him."

"Doris we have no choice in the matter. We cannot allow an officer out into the field who will lie to protect his own ass. Neither you nor I would do such a thing."

"Malachi, that is an awfully strong statement you just made about me considering how little you know me."

"You wouldn't be at that desk if it was otherwise Doris."

She just nodded as Malachi rose from the chair then left her to ponder the situation he was placing her in. He was right, she would not have even made Captain if she did not follow the leadership traits calling for honesty and integrity above all other things.

That evening Malachi found a place he could watch Belinda during her one hour of punishment as she carried ammunition cans from one side of the quad to the other with the cans becoming heavier. Once she had them across the quad, she had to take them back where she started at during the hour.

Granted it was a strain on the mind and body after the first fifteen minutes as the cans got heavier, but it was also building up the strength of the person even if they were not aware of it. Malachi remembered doing the very same detail and knew that even a modestly strengthened person could accomplish the task within the hour. If they finished too soon, the supervising officer or NCO would then have them do exercises until the time was up for that period.

He was watching her move the cans and mentally pacing her. He smiled in that unless something happened, she would finish up almost upon the hour meaning no exercises.

Malachi figured he had seen all he needed to see and started to head for his quarters when his communicator buzzed.

"Thoris here."

"Colonel Thoris, this is Fleet Communications. Sir, we have a private video call on hold for you Sir."

"Who is it from?"

"Unknown Sir, but it is via the Lancer Communications Center on Hanover Sir."

"Redirect to my office, I'm out in the quad at the moment and should be there within two minutes or so."

"Yes Sir, Comm clear."

There was very little doubt who was asking to speak to him but he also was wondering why it had taken so long since his arrival at the school and it was a well published fact he was here.

Once in his office he sat for a moment and wondered what it was gong to feel like to answer this call flashing on his monitor. He tapped accept and the image of Emma Braxton appeared.

She spoke before he had a chance.

"Malachi, I know you probably can never forgive me, but I'm sorry."

"What do you have to be sorry for Emma?"

"For never telling you about Belinda. For never giving you the chance to know your daughter."

"Emma. I will not entertain such a discussion over a video call. What ever needs to be said between us concerning our daughter will be conducted face to face. Am I clear on this?

"Perfectly clear Colonel Thoris. May I inquire as to what offense Cadet Thoris committed to garner a week's punishment?"

"And you know of this how Colonel Braxton?"

"Cadet Thoris messaged me advising that she could not have any contact outside the school during her punishment detail. She also advised me you knew of their relationship and that she was to tell me hello. That was the end of the message I received an hour ago."

"Cadet Thoris received unwanted attention in the shower facility and put a cadet in the hospital. Her punishment is not for defending herself, but in not showing restraint in doing so. And before you ask, there will be a punishment hearing against the male cadet involved once he is out of the hospital and back to duty."

Malachi had trouble keeping his composure as he looked at Emma on the screen. She was just as beautiful today as she was twenty years ago but he was not going to let her set the conditions of the discussion of their daughter after letting him discover Belinda in such a manner.

"Yes Colonel Thoris, she can have a bit of a temper at times and I suspect the cadet in question must have crossed a very delicate line with her."

Emma was quiet for a moment before speaking again.

"Malachi, there is a daily shuttle between Hanover and Denoyelles. Do I have your permission to come over and speak with you, face to face about our daughter?"

"Emma, you do not need my permission to come here. I have so many questions but as I said, I shall not consider such a discussion in this manner."

"I understand Malachi. I need to clear a few things off my desk and will shuttle over as soon as possible."

"Emma, let me know when you will arrive and my driver can pick you up at the shuttle pad. Also we have guest quarters here if you wish to spend the night. One rule as I'm sure you are aware of is that you cannot have any contact with Belinda during your stay, even if she was not on punishment."

"Yes, Malachi, I am aware of that rule. Malachi, you are looking well."

"As are you Emma. Just advise me of your schedule."

He broke the connection and leaned back in his chair. Seeing her broke old feelings to surface, feelings he was actually afraid of but in his current assignment, maybe it was time to explore the possibilities unless Belinda was unaware of attachments which Emma might have.

Collision Course

Two days later at zero eight hundred, Cadet Ronald Crossley was standing in front of Malachi's desk with Lieutenant Colonel Mifflin and Senior Lieutenant Hammerly in attendance.

"Cadet Crossley, you are here to answer to charges of Inappropriate Conduct with one Cadet Belinda Thoris in the shower facility. How do you plead?"

"Not guilty Sir."

"Cadet Crossley, do you deny touching Cadet Thoris in an inappropriate manner after she had told you at least twice she was not interested in you or engaging in any manner of sexual conduct with you?"

"Yes Sir, I deny her statements Sir."

"Since this hearing is being recorded, let it be known that I, Colonel Malachi Thoris do hereby excuse myself for any further dealings with Cadet Ronald Crossley and turn over all responsibility of such to Lieutenant Colonel Doris Mifflin, Deputy Commandant of the Fleet Marine Cadet Course. Lieutenant Colonel Mifflin, do your duty."

Mifflin stood as Crossley had a confused look on his face.

"Lieutenant Hammerly escort Cadet Crossley to the medical facility for a complete Psych examination." She ordered.

"Yes Ma'am."

Hammerly had already been briefed by both Malachi and Mifflin concerning his part in the hearing and stepped forward, took Crossley by the arm and removed him from the room. Mifflin stepped to Malachi's desk.

"Colonel Thoris, for the record Sir, you will have no further contact with Cadet Crossley or Cadet Thoris until this situation is resolved as per Fleet Marine Regulations."

"Thank you Colonel Mifflin, I understand my position in these proceedings. Please notify the Judge Advocates Office and place them on stand-by in case of need since this goes beyond Standard Operating Procedures for the school."

"I shall once I return to my office Sir."

With that Malachi turned off the recorders.

"Well Doris, do you think we've covered ourselves well enough?"

"I'd say we did. If he fails the Psych Exam, then we can turn him over to the JAG and let them deal with him. To be honest, I envision he will be on a transport to the nearest Marine Recruit Training site this time next week to finish out his enlistment contract as a Private."

"You know, it's sad to see something like this happen and I must be cursed for it to happen so soon after I take over the school."

"Colonel, I'll let you in on a secret. We have had one or two of these in every class since I've been here these past three years. The reasons vary, but the cadets still find themselves in trouble they cannot get out of. I'll have my twenty soon, and I think it is time to retire."

"I should have retired after Berkley, but I truly think I'd be lost without the Marines."

"Colonel, I can understand that but at least I have someone to keep my bed warm at night and to keep me busy outside of it when the time comes. Just thinking out loud Malachi."

"Go, take care of the JAG call, I need to think."

And think he did because he had a message the day before that Emma would be arriving later this morning. He had already instructed his driver to check shuttle arrival times and to pick up Colonel Braxton and bring her to the school. All he had to do now was read up on a new weapon system entering the Marines as he waited for her arrival.

Malachi lost track of time as he was reading up on the new Heavy Weapons system which basically duplicated an old Terrain system for firing grenades in rapid succession. He did have to slightly smile in that the concept came from the need such as during the assault on the Twelfth on Berkley and attributed the idea to one of the Sergeant's from Bravo Company.

He intended to meet Emma at the Headquarters entrance, on the steps but became so involved in reading the specifications of the weapon system it was not until his driver rapped on his door and announced Emma.

"Colonel Thoris, Colonel Braxton of the Lancers Sir."

Malachi all but jumped from his chair and went to the door to greet Emma. As she entered his office she spoke.

"Colonel Thoris, please close the door."

Once the door was closed she looked at Malachi then dropped her head to her chest.

"This was a mistake Malachi. I never should have come here."

"Well it's too late to go back now so please, sit down and let's see if we can come to some pleasant arrangement."

She sat down and he pulled a chair over so he could sit near her without the desk between them.

"Emma, let me ask some questions then you tell me why this was a mistake coming here."

"Alright."

"First of all, when did you know you were pregnant with Belinda?"

"I knew a week before you left."

"Why didn't you tell me then?"

"Because I didn't want you worrying about me or the baby. I was afraid you'd make some big deal about it. And Malachi, I knew I was leaving Keres for Hanover even before I knew I was pregnant."

"Did you intend to get pregnant?"

"No, but I knew that there was a possibility and did not take any steps to prevent it. Malachi, you are so much like Gilbert, my first husband that it scared me when I thought about you going away from Keres never to see me again. I had nothing left of Gilbert but memories and I could have a piece of you to remind me how much I cared for you and do not lie in that you also cared for me."

"Emma, I learned later in the months before Ramstein, that I was in love with you but since you had never told me how you felt, I just put that love aside and moved on."

"I tried moving on when Belinda was two. Every few years I've taken a lover and each time I came up empty, so I stopped even trying about six years ago and just focused on my assignment."

"Then what are we going to do about this?"

"Malachi I've always been so sure about myself, what I was doing and how to get things done, but with you, I'm lost."

"Do you still love me Emma?"

"Yes."

"Then I'm going to take the rest of the day off and we are going to just walk, talk and see what the day brings to us. We have so much time to make up for it's the only place I can think to start."

"Malachi, I'll not make love to you while I'm here. I'm no longer protected from becoming pregnant and I will not risk another child without a husband to help me raise it. And I'll not have you any way except natural."

"That's more that fair Emma, after all it is your body."

They spent the day off base just talking about the years they missed together. After dinner, they went back to his office and just continued talking as they tried to regain some common ground besides Belinda.

"Emma, whose idea was it for Belinda to join the Marines?"

"It was her idea. It may have been a mistake for me to give her all the articles about you but I felt it was important to know whose genes she carried. Malachi, she has been in training for this since she was eleven. When I finally accepted what she desired to do, I put her through everything I could to get her ready. She is already a Master with the swords, and I think you know her capabilities in hand to hand."

"Well she'll have to prove herself still yet just as she would if she had decided to be a Lancer. And never forget she also has your genes because she is a beauty just like her mother."

When he walked her to her quarters where his driver had deposited her bags, she kissed him hard as if she was taking him to bed.

"I've really missed you Malachi. But this is all we can have for now."

"Not a problem Emma, pleasant dreams."

The next morning they had breakfast together before she boarded the shuttle to return to Hanover. Colonel Mifflin was waiting for him when he came into his office.

"Malachi, the Docs broke Crossley's story about fifteen hundred hours. He broke like a dry twig. I had punishment on him about thirty minutes later and he left my office in care of the Military Police. It's out of our hands now."

"Doris believe me when I say I hated to put you into that situation but I feel it's not over until we hear from the Ambassador who sponsored him."

"Don't worry about it. Simon has been trying to get me in front of a priest for months and last night I told him it was time. I'm having my birth control removed today and with luck I'll retire fat as a tick with his demon child growing inside of me."

"Doris, I wish you all of the luck in the world."

End Game

The Cadet Course is six months long and on Denoyelles, the temperature is always warm even if the humidity is low except in the lush forest belt along the equator. For the cadets, the last two months are spent mostly in the field training in team, squad, and section tactics in preparation for them to one day take over a section as a Sub-Lieutenant.

Once a month Emma would transit to Denoyelles to visit Malachi without them ever venturing into the bedroom. Malachi actually had a house since previous Commandants of the school were married, and in the months following her first visit, she stayed in one of the guest bedrooms of his quarters during her visits.

They may not have ventured into the bedrooms, but the action on the living room couch often got very heated without any clothing being removed.

A week before graduation, commissioning of the Cadets, Malachi went to the Commandant of Marines with a request.

"General Cardellini, you are aware of my service record Sir, and I have never asked the service anything for myself, but I would like to ask for one thing Sir."

"You can ask Colonel Thoris."

"General Cardellini, in case you are not aware, my daughter is in the Cadet Course and will soon graduate at the top of her class. Sir, until I met her at the start of the training cycle I wasn't even aware I had a daughter, which is a long story in itself Sir, and Colonel Emmanuel Braxton of the Lancers at the Lancer Academy can verify my statement Sir."

He paused as he formed his words.

"Sir, I would appreciate it if Cadet Thoris be assigned to the Cadet Course as an instructor once she is commissioned as a Sub-Lieutenant. This will give me a short time, a couple of years before she ships out Sir."

"Has she selected a field yet?"

"Yes Sir, she has opted for Intelligence Sir.

"Have you talked to Cadet Thoris about staying at the school?"

"No Sir, except for having to deal with her during the Crossley incident, I have not spoken to her since. She is aware that I've avoided contact with her so no one could claim favoritism. Sir."

"That's right, I forgot she was the victim in that incident. Malachi, if I grant your wish be prepared for some within the system to be upset over the privilege I'll be giving you. But you are one of the few to ever wear two Medal's of Valor. I'd say you deserve the right to serve with your only child. I'll grant your request Colonel."

"Thank you Sir. I've taken enough of your time Sir."

Emma arrived the day before graduation and over dinner Malachi told her what he had done. Emma told him if that was how he wanted to be able to see his daughter on a regular basis, then she had no problem with it. Then Malachi did the unexpected.

"Emma, marry me."

"Why? I mean why now?"

"Because I'd like to ask you to retire and just be my wife."

"Malachi, I will marry you but I will not retire as long as Belinda is here and let me be clear on this, she will not live in this house with you during her assignment here, but in her own quarters so she will have a normal social life."

"If you'll marry but not retire, will you request transfer to an assignment here on Denoyelles?"

"No. I will continue to come over as I have and you can even come to Hanover at times, but you need this time alone with

Belinda without my influence. Maybe it does not make sense at the moment but it will in time."

Malachi just looked at her thinking she was probably right.

"So Colonel Thoris, when would you like to get married?"

"I'll leave that to you Emma."

"Since I have my dress uniform with me and I have a week before having to be back at my desk. We can get married anytime you want after graduation so Belinda can be present."

"Okay, I'll arrange for a Chaplin in the morning."

"That's fine Malachi my love, now eat up and after the dishes are done, you can have me for dessert tonight."

"Emma, I do think I have ate my full then."

Emma laughed as she stood and began clearing the table with Malachi helping. She decided she could wash the dishes in the morning before getting ready for the graduation ceremony.

Belinda was surprised when she saw her mother sitting on the reviewing stand with her father. When Malachi spoke to the class before they came forward to receive their commissioning papers, he introduced Emma as Belinda's mother but never spoke of him being her father.

The Commandant of Marines was present to swear in the Cadets as officers of the Fleet Marine Force and handed each individual their commissioning papers which included their orders for their next assignment. Of the one hundred and three that started the course, ninety-five would graduate. One lost for disciplinary action and four injured with two of those returning for the next class. Malachi and Emma shook each individuals hands as they passed across the reviewing stand with Belinda also receiving a hug from her mother.

Malachi watched Belinda as she returned to her chair to await the others moving to receive their papers and the look he saw on her face was one of confusion as she opened her folder to see her orders. He never smiled as he returned her gaze but he did take Emma's hand for only a moment, which brought a smile to Belinda's face.

When Malachi dismissed the class, the cheers were loud then as the class began to congratulate each other and compare orders, the reviewing stand emptied with Malachi and Emma escorting the Commandant of Marines to his transport. Before he entered his vehicle, the Commandant spoke to Emma.

"Colonel Braxton, I've heard a lot about you over the years and it is an honor to finally meet you. You have done great things with the Lancer Academy and maybe once you have some time on your hands, you can offer some advice in improving ours. Colonel Thoris don't take that wrong as you have done a great job with this first class and have made some fine recommendations on improving the course, but it never hurts to get another opinion."

"No Sir it doesn't." Malachi responded.

"General thank you for the compliment, but I believe politics between the Marines and Lancers might prevent some of the ideas I have offered to the Lancer command might not make it past Fleet review Sir."

"Considering how many former Marines are now serving in the Lancers, I think it is time to merge as many ideas as possible so when working together in the field, there is less confusion to deal with. Now one last thing."

He paused for a second.

"Intelligence informs me that the two of you have reignited the flames which brought Lieutenant Thoris into this world. Don't the two of you need to make the arrangement more permanent?"

Malachi laughed before responding.

"General Cardellini, we intend to do that this afternoon once our daughter has the time to say goodbye to her classmates."

Cardellini laughed then pointed to Malachi.

"With the separation the two of you have to deal with at the moment, Colonel Thoris if you even hint at retiring, I'll have you drawn and quartered then sewn back together so you can continue here at the school. There are things in the air, in the system I cannot divulge at the moment, but your not leaving, even if it is for such a lovely woman as the Colonel here."

"Thank you for the compliment General." Emma spoke as Malachi was trying not to laugh at the General's comments.

Cardellini once more took Emma's hand.

"Thank the Saints that Lieutenant Thoris took after you in the looks department Colonel. Both of you have a fair day and Colonel Thoris, consider yourself on leave until Colonel Braxton has to return to Hanover. That's an order."

"Order received and accepted Sir. Thank you."

As soon as the General departed, Malachi had his driver take him and Emma out into Denoyelles City where they found simple wedding rings for that afternoon.

When they returned, they found Belinda sitting outside his office patiently waiting for their return. Malachi indicated for her to follow them as they entered the office. Belinda spoke first.

"Father....."

She never had a chance to complete the sentence as her mother shut her down.

"Lieutenant Thoris, under no circumstance will you refer to Colonel Thoris in any familiar manner outside his quarters, especially in his office with the door still open. Do I make myself clear Lieutenant?"

"Yes Colonel Braxton, my apologizes Colonel Thoris, I forgot myself for a moment, it'll never happen again."

Emma closed the door to Malachi's office then picked up where she left off.

"Belinda, I said what I said and loud enough that if anyone heard me, they would know that you are not getting any special privileges just because you are the Colonel's daughter. Never allow anyone to think that and you'll go far."

"Yes Ma'am. But I have a problem with my orders."

"What's the problem with your orders? Malachi asked.

"Sir, they say I'm to be your Aide de Camp for a period not less than two years. What of my Intelligence courses Sir?"

"Aide de Camp? Since when does a Colonel have an Aide de Camp?" Emma asked no one in particular.

"Let me see your orders." Malachi instructed.

Belinda handed the orders over and once Malachi read them he handed them to Emma before speaking to Belinda.

"Sub-Lieutenant Thoris, your orders also state that you have thirty days shore leave effective today. You will also take quarter's in the BOQ, so I suggest you go deal with that unless you have done that already. Then at sixteen hundred hours, you will report to my personal quarters to witness the marriage of myself to your mother. Do you have any questions concerning my instructions Lieutenant?"

A big smile appeared on Belinda's face.

"No Sir, I do not have a problem with the orders Sir."

"Good, and maybe by the time you are off shore leave, we'll have the questions of your assignment dealt with. You are dismissed Lieutenant."

"Aye-Aye Sir."

As Belinda exited his office, Malachi punched his intercom and asked for Colonel Mifflin to come see him. When she arrived Malachi advised her of General Cardellini's orders in reference to leave with Emma and that they were getting married that afternoon. He would only be in his office today to clear a few

136

things off his desk, then the school was hers until he came off leave.

The wedding that afternoon went off without a hitch as Belinda stood with her mother as the Maid of Honor, and Malachi had Major Pickering, his Operations Officer as Best Man.

Emma suggest they honeymoon in the Southern Alps of Hanover where the Lancers had a resort. That evening they caught the night shuttle to Hanover and it was after midnight before they consummated their marriage.

Emma asked Malachi if he wanted another child which gave him pause since they were both well into their forties until Emma advised him she was in perfect shape and it was not unknown for Centaurian females to birth children into their fifties.

Malachi told Emma that Belinda was enough at his age and even then he was still getting used to the idea of having a daughter. Emma laughed and told him how lucky he was not to have had to deal with Belinda when she hit puberty.

They had ten days in the Alps before Emma had to return to her desk. They decided that at least once a month, either Emma would come to him for a weekend or he would go to her. It took some time before they settled on a basic schedule subject to change as per duty requirements.

Malachi was back a week with Belinda still on her shore leave. He was taking an early morning jog around the compound as he had since he arrived and saw Belinda exiting Hammerly's quarters with them kissing at his door before she turned for her own quarters. Malachi felt lucky she lived away from him instead of one of the apartments in his direction. He paused and waited until she went into her quarters before continuing his run.

Belinda joined Malachi for lunch in the Staff Dining Facility and they talked about what he considered her duties would be as his Aide de Camp without bringing up how she spent her night. She was old enough to make her own decisions and if

Hammerly was one of them, so be it as he felt Hammerly was a fine officer and should soon be promoted to Captain.

Two days before Belinda was to report for duty, Malachi was ordered to report to Fleet Marine Headquarters. He left the meeting with a new Table of Organization for the Cadet Course along with the single Starburst insignia of a Brigadier General on his collars. Malachi also left with the feeling the Fleet Marine General Staff was a touch insane.

He had barely entered his office when he had a video call from a Lancer terminal which he figured was Emma. He was correct but not about the reason she was calling.

"What the Seven Hell's of Sparta is going on over there Malachi?"

"You want to explain that a bit better Emma? I have no idea what you are talking about."

"I just received orders to Fleet Marine Headquarters as the Lancer Liaison Officer effective immediately. Did you have anything to do with this assignment?"

"No Emma, I did not and would not have entertained such without talking to you first."

"Then it must be General Cardellini who came up with this bright idea. By the way, those Starbursts look good on your uniform."

"Honey, all I can say is I think insanity is running rampant at Fleet Headquarters. Since we both have to accept our orders, when do you think you'll transit over?"

"They are giving me a week. How about sending Belinda over to help me pack up my quarters since she still has things here."

"I'll get her on this evenings shuttle although it might interfere with her love life."

"What?"

"Don't say anything to her, but I saw her leaving Lieutenant Hammerly's quarters a few days ago just before daylight and they shared a long kiss at his door before she went to her quarters. I have not said a thing to either of them since she is well over the age of consent."

"Damn. He must be special if she gave him her gift."

"He's a fine officer Emma."

"Alright, send her over and I'll stay quiet about her private life because as you said, she is certainly old enough to make that decision by herself."

Sunsets

Since the location of the Cadet Course was within the Fleet Marine Headquarters area, this made it easy for Emma to live with Malachi with his driver taking her to her office and picking her up until General Cardellini had a vehicle and driver assigned to her.

Belinda became a common fixture in their quarters as Malachi and her closed the years of being separated with Belinda spending her duty hours working on computer courses for her Intelligence field requirements when she was not running errands for him as his Aide de Camp.

Emma had been on Denoyelles for almost six months when they were having a family dinner in quarters when she asked the question of Belinda that shocked her.

"So Belinda, what are your plans concerning Lieutenant Hammerly since he is due to be transferred soon?"

"Mother, I'm not sure what you mean?"

"Well daughter of mine, you have all but moved into his bedroom, so is it serious or just having fun?"

Belinda looked at her mother then Malachi before looking back at Emma.

"Mother has it been so obvious?"

"No, but you forget I too started out in Intelligence. Well, answer my question."

Belinda moved some vegetables around on her plate with a fork before answering.

"Marriage is impracticable considering he is Infantry and I will be assigned an Intelligence post later on. Mom, I think I understand you even better now than before. Do I give up one dream for another or just wait to see where life leads me? As hard as Jonathon can be on the parade deck, he is a soft and gentle man. When I told him I had never been with a man in a carnal way, he

140

pushed me away, told me it was not his place to take that gift. I didn't give him much choice after that as I stripped and told him to either take me to bed or I'd stand in his doorway and scream my head off."

Malachi could not contain his laughter as he envisioned Hammerly trying to stifle such screams. Emma had a different reaction.

"You didn't!"

"Yes mother, I was determined that if any man would have me my first time it would be him. Too be honest I've had a crush on him from nearly day one of the course. And I think I made the right choice in picking him as the experience was all I expected it to be and more."

Malachi suddenly stopped laughing and stood up.

"Excuse me ladies but I just realized this is not a subject a father needs to be hearing between his daughter and her mother."

"Sit back down husband of mine as you might as well hear this too."

She waited until Malachi sat back down.

"Belinda I gave away my virginity a lot younger than you are now and never looked back as I enjoyed several lovers until I met Gilbert Braxton. He turned my world inside out. But his death turned me cold inside with no desire to take another lover until I saw your father sitting in a shot up bunker bleeding from several holes in his body yet still commanding the battle."

Emma took a sip of tea.

"But I put him out of my mind other than he excited me at that moment in time. Then over a year later we met on Keres and I found he still excited me but unlike in my youth, I paced him and myself until we finally took the final step and found out how well we fit together. Did I love him at the time? No, but before he left, before I knew I was pregnant with you, I was in love with him.

141

But I never told him exactly how I felt as I was not going to go through the pain again of loosing someone I loved as I had with Gilbert. I let him leave Keres without knowing I truly loved him and that I was carrying you."

She just paused for a moment before continuing.

"Your father was in a Lazarus tank and you were two years old when I took another lover for a single night but it was far from fulfilling. I took several more over the years but it was all the same. The sex itself might have been good, but it just did not fulfill me as your father did so I just stopped wasting my time. Now in a way, you brought us back together because if you had gone into the Lancers, I would never have came over to see your father as I was afraid of facing him and the fact I denied him knowledge of his child for all those years."

"Mother where is this heading?"

"Belinda it does not matter who really fulfills you but do not let them go, and if they have to leave or you leave them because of duty, tell them how you feel, then move on. You never know what the universe will present to you tomorrow."

"Mother as convoluted as that sounds, it actually makes sense. Thank you."

Later in bed, Malachi told Emma he had made the right decision in not asking her for another child as he was ill prepared to raise one.

At the end of Belinda's two years, she was sent to the Fleet's Intelligence School to complete her education. Hammerly had left for the Ninth Marines to take over an Infantry Company before her time was up as Malachi's Aide de Camp. Her own love life slowed as she focused on her duties, then the schooling before her next assignment.

Belinda was posted to the Fleet Heavy Cruiser as the Marine Intelligence Officer attachment to the Cruiser's heavy Infantry Company.

At the end of Malachi's four years as Commandant of the Cadet Course and making several critical improvements to the course, he was transferred to Fleet Marine Headquarters into the Operations office.

Emma finally retired and became a homemaker for Malachi to return to each evening. Belinda returned to Denoyelles as a Captain and was assigned to the Intelligence Office at Headquarters.

Jonathon Hammerly had a very successful assignment with the Ninth and was promoted to Major as the Ninth's Operation Officer. Malachi noticed that Belinda had suitors but it seemed she had taken her mother's advice to heart and according to gossip, she rarely took a man to her bed. According to Emma, Belinda still had a major piece of her heart tied to Hammerly.

Malachi arranged for Hammerly to return to Denoyelles and the Cadet Course as its Operations Officer, then arranged for Belinda to learn of his return before he actually arrived.

Six months later Malachi gave his daughter away in marriage to Jonathon Hammerly.

Over the next eight years, Malachi held various positions to include a three year tour as a Sector Commander before returning to Denoyelles as Deputy Commandant of the Fleet Marine Force.

Emma played grandmother to the two sons Belinda gave Jonathon as both of them advanced in rank.

Malachi became Commandant of the Fleet Marine Force when the Commandant was severely injured in an aircar crash. Malachi lead the Fleet Marines for four years before he said he had enough and retired.

In his last official act as Commandant he took advantage of his position and sent both Jonathon and Belinda to Keres to non-combat assignments as he and Emma also went to Keres and a home he had arranged for their retirement.

They spent their lives watching their grandsons grow and leave to join the fleet as they watched the sunset over Keres.

About The Author

Leon Michaels is the author of several novels and short stories that reflect his twenty-three years of military service. Michaels enlisted in the Marine Corps in 1970 and has memberships in the Veterans of Foreign Wars, the American Legion, the Disabled American Veterans organizations, NRA, and Rotary International. In 1971, he married his high school sweetheart, raised three daughters and has three grandsons. He calls Creek County, Oklahoma home.

Made in the USA
Columbia, SC
17 April 2019